janicemuir.com

FORGET ME NOT

–

LOSING MY PARTNER TO ALZHEIMER'S DEMENTIA

NOVEL ABOUT LOVE LOST

by *JANICE MUIR*

FORGET ME NOT
- LOSING MY PARTNER TO ALZHEIMER'S DEMENTIA *by* JANICE MUIR

Forget Me Not –

Losing My Partner to Alzheimer's Dementia novel about love lost

© Janice Muir 2022

National Library of Australia Cataloguing-in-Publication(pbk)

Author:	Muir, Janice Author
Title:	Forget Me Not
	– Losing my partner to Alzheimer's Dementia
ISBN:	9780987401175 (paperback)
ISBN:	9780987401199 (E-Book; E-Pub)
Subjects:	Biography, Self Help Techniques

Published by Janice Muir
Self-Published I Believe I Achieve

Book Cover Story: Photographer Sue Seaby, South Australia

As my partner and I were driving passed the Myponga Reservoir in South Australia there is a small opening that meets Main South Road, and it was at this point I was admiring the ever-changing colors of the sky. I was soaking up the beauty aligned to the fabric of my soul and then spotted the most aww inspiring view to the naked eye. I asked my partner to pull over; I needed this photo I could feel it at my core. There was a deep need to take this photo. Without question here I was standing next to the fence. The car is stopped it was quiet and still. There was the most beautiful picture with all the elements that held true to my heart of a fairy tale I had dreamed from a little child unfolding before my very eyes. I took photo after photo of the color changes and position. I said to my partner as I got back in the car feeling elated to have captured the essence of such beauty that thus will be a book cover. A book cover of the most beautiful love story just like a fairy tale with the moon and the star... It was a gift to me then as it is still to me to this day. I never knew it was not to be my fairy tale, however the universe unfolded to be able to share to someone else's love story whatever the tale. Forever grateful for my callings, no journey is by accident, everything has its calling.

Much love Sue Seaby

photography.shetime.com.au
shetime.com.au

Self-Publishing via Ingram Spark
I Believe I Achieve – Janice Muir

Graphic Design & Artwork
Astrid Kuenne (Your Brand Management)
www.yourbrandmanagement.com.au

Acknowledgement:

A special thank you to Sue Seaby, who gave of her time
and shared comments and feedback for all the Awareness
Wisdom Awakeners pages. Her valued input was such a
blessing having worked in this industry and she understood
the situations. At times aghast at the impact yet very intuitive
to share constructive comments to help me on this writing
journey.

Table of Contents

Dedication

To every family member who is witnessing
another member walk this pathway.

Always remember your perspective
is an outside view.

The family member cannot help
things that are happening.

If you feel hate, anger, or frustration
then it is because you do not understand
what is happening.

Lift your judgment on the situation,
have compassion and an open heart.

*For one day, it,
could be you,
that needs that Care.*

Be Supportive

Let Judgement Go

Acknowledgements

Janice has written a poignant raw and powerful story.

This book was hard to put down it held my attention.

The process of grief is letting go of a
person as you knew them.

While each person has a different version of being touched
by Alzheimer's disease it is a steep learning curve.
Needing to remember how frightening
their world must be too.

There are moments of connection and laughter
that can make your day.

Thank you, Janice, for your honesty and
providing resources to others.

I wish you and your daughter all the best.

Christine Bailey
Brisbane

We experience many little deaths in our lifetimes. None so heart-wrenching though, as seeing the mind of the person you love fade away right before your eyes.

To lose that connection and not be recognised, and indeed to no longer recognise the person you knew and loved is anathema[1]. The body is still here but the person you knew is gone.

The heartache and grief for all concerned is profound. Tears fell down my cheeks when Janice shared the following... *"I had already conditioned myself to fall out of love with Barry as a way to make it easier for me to cope."*

As a Registered Nurse who ran a rest home for 6 years, I know this pain and this book will help those moving through this experience for they will recognize themselves in this poignant story of love found and lost, unrelenting stressors and the frailty of our relationships.

Pat Armitstead

RGN, Dip Ed, FCN NSW

Email: Pat@joyology.co.nz

Website: www.joyology.co.nz

---

1   Anathema, in the form of something like a curse nothing negative however with lack of believe in God or higher Power, Barry never allowed his belief to have any influence over him and so never believed there was a God. So, to look upon his demise and see he longer recognised myself or daughter it was a hard loss of connection to witness.

This would not have been an easy book to write.

Janice opens the door and shares her journey with living with her partner diagnosed at an early age with Alzheimer's Dementia. It is an emotional, raw, and hard journey.

Yet it still leaves us with hope. Janice's story is a deep look into the effects this hard disease has on family when a loved one is diagnosed with Alzheimer's Dementia. The journey held me enthralled as Janice shared the milestones of discovery and the slow deterioration of Barry.

I found the comprehensive introduction valuable in providing a background to a very confronting illness. It gives the reader a foundation for the story to follow.

Thank you, Janice for your very honest sharing of a significant part of your life's journey.

Trish Springsteen

Email: trish@trishspringsteen.com

Website: www.trishspringsten.com

Janice Muir has written a most useful, practical, and compassionate guide to understanding the pain of love and loss with Alzheimer's Dementia. It is a wonderful guide for others living with their loved one's dementia story. This book is a deep, moving journey through the complexities of loving, living and compassion around living with dementia as Janice sees it. You have shared your life, your experiences, and your wisdom. I have no doubt this book will touch many lives.

It certainly has mine.

Di Riddell Confidence Coach,
Speaker and author of 'Speak Out'
Email: di@diriddell.com
Website: www.diriddell.com

FORGET -ME-NOT by JANICE MUIR.

"That's it; I've read enough of it," I told myself. But unfortunately, I had only read half page of Janice Muir's manuscript introductions to "Forget-me-not".

I felt compelled to stop reading it because all I wanted was to hold the hard copy in my hands; I could immediately tell this was the kind of story I must read.

I have experienced just one hour of the type of anxiety Janice describes, and when it happened, I was shocked; I did not know what to make of it, and I put the experience out of my mind.

Twenty years ago, my soul-mate husband of thirty years, at that time, had said to me, "Who are you? You are not my wife!"

Now I wish to learn more about what causes dementia and how I can prepare myself and stop making unnecessary mistakes should life strike a blow to my soulmate, or vice-versa, for my soulmate to deal with me.

My congratulations, dear Janice Muir, for sharing and educating us with the telling of a painful period in your life. Just by reading a short paragraph, I can tell your sensitive heart is here for us. Sharing is caring.

With love and respect.

Livia York,

Author/Poetess

Email: phoenix@liviayork.com

Website: www.liviayork.com

Janice and I met on the net via a mutual friend, and you have shared a lot with me on my journey, as a runner as well.

I gained some insight to my long distance running from the power of visioning. I have thoroughly enjoyed your latest book. It has allowed me to know you better from what you have shared, and I loved reading your story and truly honoured to be part of it.

Yes, some parts of the book were hard to grasp as we never know how hard things can be for everyone's experience however your story helped me understand my own situation with my gran. Devastating as it was for her demise. My gran was 81 in age she also witnessed her second youngest son pass with the sudden onset of cancer. My gran struggled with this news however she passed around 2 yrs after her diagnosis. Having witnessed the impact of cancer for my uncle which impacted all the family and my gran's demise seemed hard to understand back in 2006 as I was only a young adult when it all started to happen, so your book gave me a greater perspective I could appreciate what she was witnessing during her time. This disease truly does impact on individuals and family as it hits us hard when we truly come to understand what is happening to our loved ones. Your courage and experience allowed me to feel a deeper connection to you as your shared the rawness of this journey you have experienced.

I feel it is such a brave thing to do; to be so vulnerable and to open your heart and allow the world in to know so much about you and your loved ones. Your story is one to be commended as it has truly amazed me what you have witnessed and still be here today to share.

I am not sure I would have the courage you have expressed, and I want to say a special thank you for sharing your stories with me. Well done and sincere Thank you. Dolene

My dear internet friend I know, like and trust. x

Dolene from Scotland

*** **** ***

Janice has written several books about her life experiences and knowledge she gained from them. Her generous nature allowed her to share her experiences with us. Many of us carry our wounds inside us, unable to articulate them nor are we willing to share them with others. We learn from each other and from each other's stories. Dealing with Alzheimer is a daunting problem facing more and more of us, Janice had to deal with it at a younger age and during a time when few Doctors knew about it and even fewer lay people. It was a disease that was not known nor understood; Janice had to identify it in her partner; deal with it daily and try and find a place where he would be taken care of. This book is about a journey of heartbreak and discovery; and the generosity of one woman doing her best for her family. Janice was able to articulate her journey, showing empathy, humour, and deep sadness for what was, and loss of what could have been.

Longtime and close friend
Susan Luong-Van

Prologue

Lisa Cobb

Barry is what I call a true "Territorian[2]." - What you saw is what you got! He called a spade a spade. You knew when you asked Barry something you would get a straight answer and knew exactly where you stood. There were no pretences about him.

He had an endearing cheeky personality and made everyone feel like they were special. He always took the time to talk to everyone and acknowledge their situation.

Barry was a very clever man and humble about his abilities. However, was always willing to share his knowledge if asked.

When Janice first shared that Barry was diagnosed with this debilitating disease, I was speechless. I could not myself fathom how a clever man as he was could now be with little to no memory of his life. It was one of the hardest things to witness and the journey that Janice was on, truly one that I was not sure how I would have coped and managed.

Barrys ability was gentleman like, and he managed twenty-two apprentices as one of the foreman's when he worked in the Power Station in Darwin where I met him.

---

2 A person who is native to or resident in the Northern Territory

The power of the story is yes what pain was witnessed and I assisted where I could on this journey, however it was also the loss of the man from his knowledgeable soul to now be diagnosed with this illness.

A sad time for the Janice and her daughter.

He really was A True Gentleman

Lisa Cobb

Introduction

The Identification

Do you know how the brain works?
Do you know what causes the brain to act the way it does?

What makes it function well for some and not for others?

What on earth is Alzheimer's Dementia?

This sent me on a huge learning curb, not only for me however my daughter as well. I didn't even know what it really meant initially.

I only thought it was for old folk and something that others get; I was not prepared for the impact this would have on my life nor my daughter's life for that matter. Let alone anyone else in our surrounds that knew my partner and witnessed the demise in his persona.

There were many more questions I faced and had to understand what Alzheimer's was about when I was first introduced to this part of life that I was witnessed in my then 30-year partnership with my Barry.

As funny at it sounded at the time the saying of the acronym C.R.A.F.T (Can't Remember A F'ing Thing), it was no longer a funny comment now, that I was witnessing this in front of me.

Little did I realise along with the nil comprehension of what this journey would entail whilst I was witnessing Alzheimer's Dementia with my partner Barry.

Some technical information to broaden your awareness that I did not have when this all first started back in 1996. For me, the knowledge and depth of what they now know was not readily available and nor did I have a need to go looking for it. Now here I was attending sessions to truly gain an understanding of what was happening to my partner and what I had to manage and cope with.

A very scary place to witness and to be right in front of you to manage and care for.

What I share here is from the Dementia Australia website: https://www.dementia.org.au/

Key facts and statistics *Updated January 2022*

Australian statistics

- Dementia is the **second leading cause of death** of Australians. 1

- Dementia is the **leading cause of death** for women. 2

- In 2022, there are an **estimated 487,500 Australians** living with dementia. Without a medical breakthrough, the number of people with dementia is expected to **increase to almost 1.1 million by 2058**. 3

- In 2022, there are an **estimated 28,800 people** with younger onset dementia, expected to rise to **29,350 people by 2028** and **41,250 people by 2058**. This can include people in their 30s, 40s and 50s. 3

- In 2022, it is estimated that **almost 1.6 million** people in Australia are involved in the care of someone living with dementia. 4

- Approximately **70% of people with dementia** live in the community. 5

- **More than two-thirds** (68.1%) of aged care residents have moderate to severe cognitive impairment. 6

Dementia risk reduction

Being brain healthy is relevant at any age, whether you are young, old, or in between. However, it is particularly important once you reach middle age as this is when changes start to occur in the brain.

While we cannot change getting older, genetics or family history, scientific research suggests that changing certain health and lifestyle habits may make a big difference to reducing or delaying your risk of developing dementia.

There are 12 recommendations for reducing risk for cognitive decline released by the World Health Organisation: 7

1. Be physically active
2. Stop smoking
3. Eat a balanced diet, like the Mediterranean diet
4. Drink alcohol in moderation
5. Cognitive training
6. Be socially active
7. Look after your weight
8. Manage any hypertension
9. Manage any diabetes
10. Manage any cholesterol
11. Manage depression
12. Look after your hearing and manage hearing loss.

Dementia prevalence in Australia

The prevalence data research for dementia in Australia is conducted and regularly updated by Dementia Australia. Detailed information about dementia prevalence can be found here.

What is dementia?

Dementia is the term used to describe the symptoms of a large group of illnesses which cause a progressive decline in a person's functioning. It is a broad term used to describe a loss of memory, intellect, rationality, social skills, and physical functioning. There are many types of dementia including Alzheimer's disease, vascular dementia, frontotemporal dementia, and Lewy body disease. Dementia can happen to anybody, but it is more common after the age of 65.

Who is Dementia Australia?

Dementia Australia is the source of trusted information, education, and services for the estimated half a million Australians living with dementia, and the almost 1.6 million people involved in their care. We advocate for positive change and support vital research.

We are here to support people impacted by dementia, and to enable them to live as well as possible.

No matter how you are impacted by dementia or who you are, we are here for you.

Dementia Australia, the new voice of Alzheimer's Australia, is the national peak body for people, of all ages, living with all forms of dementia, their families, and carers. It provides advocacy, support services, education, and information.

1. Australian Bureau of Statistics (2020) Causes of Death, Australia, 2019 (cat. No. 3303.0)

2. Australian Institute of Health and Welfare, Dementia Snapshot, July 2020

3. Dementia Australia (2018) Dementia Prevalence Data 2018-2058, commissioned research undertaken by NATSEM, University of Canberra

4. Based on Dementia Australia's analysis of the following publications – M. Kostas et al. (2017) National Aged Care Workforce Census and Survey – The Aged Care Workforce, 2016, Department of Health; Dementia Australia (2018) Dementia Prevalence Data 2018–2058, commissioned research undertaken by NATSEM, University of Canberra; Alzheimer's Disease International and Karolinska Institute (2018), Global estimates of informal care, Alzheimer's Disease International; Access Economics (2010) Caring Places: planning for aged care and dementia 2010–2050

5. Australian Institute of Health and Welfare (2012) Dementia in Australia

6. Royal Commission into Aged Care Quality and Safety, Research Paper 8 - International and National Quality and Safety Indicators for Aged Care, 2020, p161.

7. World Health Organisation, Risk Reduction of Cognitive Decline and Dementia, 2020.

Downloadable facts and statistics

- **The key facts and statistics published on this page are also available as a pdf file.**

Download the key facts and statistics pdf file - updated January 2022

- **The economic cost of dementia in Australia 2016-2056**

The cited report National Centre for Social and Economic Modelling NATSEM (2016) Economic Cost of Dementia in Australia 2016-2056 is available here.

Introduction cont...

Barry was not a hypochondriac, in fact I don't recall him being ever sick as such, a good strong constitute kept him afloat and living life the best he could and knew how to. Neither of us were sick kind of people we had the odd cold and sore finger here and there however to be sick was out of our natural persona, overall, always a good bill of health.

So, when I discovered that Barry seemed to be suffering from a lack of swift recollection of information, which was totally converse to whom I knew him to be, I could be pardoned for seeming to have reacted a little bit.

Getting my partner to the doctors was a considerable feat after a few unignorable incidents that nearly made me have kittens. He did not see anything wrong, nor did he accept that there was any need to consult an expert. On numerous occasions, he had insisted that I needed the doctor more than he.

Why was I so persistent in keeping at him for an appointment?

My daughter and I had witnessed several changes in Barry. We didn't require the professional assistance of a medical expert to discern that something was amiss with him. Yes, physically, he looked healthy. Not once did he raise any alarm about his appearance either.

One could understand I was relatively shocked to discover his cognitive functions were quite impaired. I was not a doctor; neither was my daughter; however, we didn't have to be told by anyone we needed to consult with a recognised specialist. Something was not functioning in a normal manner. So naturally it was to be seen by a doctor that would settle all questions and merely we could be on our way. How wrong I was to be!

Do not misquote me. Of the truth, every human loses some modicum of knowledge now and then as regards the location of items. We forget some random pieces of information and may require some inconstant, involuntary jolt to the brain to recall such information. It was quite different, this time. In every right, Barry's health challenge was an entirely different case. At first, I shrugged and discarded my fears every moment a niggling thought pegged the onset of his ailment back in my mind. I barely took cognisance of it until it persistently kept appearing in different forms, at different times. I knew I had to act upon my fears before he took a turn for the worse.

Perhaps you wouldn't be so quick to berate my desire to rally behind him when I share his story with you. Barry had always been a finicky human all his life. He had an eye for details. Imagine such nonpareil astuteness of a human who understood the inner workings of every engine. It never mattered where or when he met them. All those years ago, he could close his eyes and name an engine's mechanical components, with punctilious consideration of its type, year of manufacture and engineering limitations. He understood every intricate part of engineering, be it complex or basic, fundamental, or convoluted. He made it look easy. Sometimes, I often dubbed him a show-off, however his actions weren't boastful.

He was just brainy, and he existed in a whole different world where mediocrity would never take root. Of course, I would be a chronic liar if I were to claim he never wowed me with his brilliance. As a tour coach-driver who worked for several years, it was quite understandable that Barry's job was quite taxing. Barry was required to pack luggage into much smaller areas on coach bins, as one of the requirements of his job description. Whenever he was on the job, Barry had to be accurate enough not to lose track of his actions. A job that he delivered on every single time. Then as life would share it was an out of the blue moment, when Barry could barely pack a trailer. The same man who was the most informed in the family. The same man who could whip up any piece of information from nothingness. I kept wondering how Barry deteriorated so quickly. All the while, the question ate at me, and I couldn't provide a credible answer.

Mathematically, Barry was very apt with numbers and calculations. Also, he was able to draw out technical components of anything he would make on a milling machine or lathe. Barry understood the logistics of long division, but when confronted with short division calculations, he could not see how the answer was derived. He understood the micrometre of an inch. He could conveniently relate that to the smallest shaving of steel from an inside measurement of any wheel he was making on a lathe or milling machine. Think about it... a micron meter of an inch using vernier callipers. Not everyone's average use of a mechanical tool[3].

---

3   Vernier Caliper, instrument for making very accurate linear measurements. It utilizes two graduated scales: a main scale like that on a ruler and an especially graduated auxiliary scale, the vernier, that slides parallel to the main scale and enables readings to be made to a fraction of a division on the main scale. Vernier calipers are widely used in scientific laboratories and in manufacturing for quality control measurements

This journey took me on several huge learning curves: one of understanding and the other, of complete and utter awareness of what the capabilities of our bodies were and namely the brain what its total cognitive function could and couldn't do. Also, the journey made me ask questions about the events ongoing in my mind. I wanted to know every single action of the brain. I was interested in every activity, from its operations to its problem-solving tendencies. When I had to watch my partner's cognitive abilities and functions deteriorate helplessly, I asked more questions about the human mind. What is happening in our brain and what completes our brain to be non-coherent to want to perform. Why and what caused this disruption.

The following pages will share a journey of an event that occurred and what transpired as I coped with dealing with an illness that affects the mind, and then eventually shuts the body down.

At the time that I wrote this book, first draft back in 2016, there was no known cure for this health scare. At that time, experimental drugs and mind-awakening techniques required to combat the disease were in their early stages of testing and may have been for ages. It's a complex area of the body to manage. Alzheimer's had the authorities baffled for a long time why and what was happening to those that were misfortunate to have this occur. My personal feeling is the amount of sugar that is absorbed into our body is crystalised in the mind more than we can give it credit for. The sad part is dementia and onset Alzheimer's is beginning in 40 years old and it's only a matter of time to be in younger generations.

My partner was 62 when diagnosed and passed when he was 67. This is a journey of the impact it had on me and the upheaval and impact that was witnessed not only to the patient Barry however to my 15 yrs old daughter as well[4].

Dealing with Alzheimer's disease and dementia is not an easy job. Unfortunately, a lot of humans suffer from the hold of these health challenges every day. Some people lose their lives to these health issues eventually. More so the body breaks down from other area's they don't die of Alzheimer's Dementia; heart failure is more likely or other parts of the body break down.

In honour of my partner who lost his life to a heart attack as the body broke down, he is remembered for the journey that Alzheimer's shared with myself and daughter.

For ever at peace Barry Muir Dec 1930 – Sept 2002.

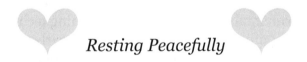

Resting Peacefully

---

4   Please note for the privacy of the family members other than Barry and the associated close friends who were part of this journey there will be no actual names mentioned. None of the information shared is fictious it's a raw encounter of events that took place.

Awareness Wisdom Awakeners

◊ Be mindful of the repetition of the same questions.

◊ It is possibly a long slow degeneration of illness to manage once it is detected.

◊ Being clever does not mean you will be smarter that you are safe from this illness – always many factors to be considered.

◊ Knowledge is everything; retaining sensible knowledge is what counts.

◊ No one fit detection for us all; it's the varying degrees of our life that impacts us.

◊ You will notice that the little things become bigger in the early detection.

◊ Being patient is a hard practice in early stages, it takes time to digest what happens in front of you and its different for everybody remember no one fit for all.

Forward

by Sue Seaby

I have loved reading the journey of Janice and Barry, it is like I was there every step of the way feeling into every moment. Having experienced working in Aged Care I resonated with the intimate moments and glimpses that Janice speaks of in this book. I invite every person to read this book because you never know who along this journey called life, you will meet or know and even yourself will have this diagnosis one day too. Do you know how the brain works?

Janice and Barry's story gives insights to the joys, pains and defining moments of the journey with Dementia from the beginning to the saddest point, the end. It is not every day you get to know the finer details of someone else's journey which may even become one that you later identify with. The love, the compassion, the patience, the fears, the joys, they are all here in this book. Come on this journey with Janice and Barry and get to know them for more than the diagnosis, find the compassion in your hearts for those that do receive the diagnosis and learn from another's journey giving yourself insight and knowledge along the journey that you too may experience.

From my experience working in Aged Care in many roles for 14 years I can speak as Janice does from personal experience that judgment is necessary for the care of someone and not in the life of someone. The polarity of judgment is so often seen, in the saddest times as I have witnessed many times during this career. Families rally and families fight, what they do not see is what I see. They are all fighting to hold onto every moment as if it were the last. Every glimpse of lucidity, families grieve not celebrate as their loved one slips into a darkness where they know they will never find them again. The pain and the grief are enormous watching a loved one fade away, and with white knuckles they cling to every moment. With the very next breathe it can also bring frustration, anger misunderstandings and confusion as the journey is so unknown to many that begin to experience Dementia with a loved one.

For me personally I got to witness everything from the ultimate happiness and joy of celebrating someone's life to the sadness of their passing. Each journey is completely different with each family dynamics unfolding, what is consistent is the loss of the persons details of their life. As they age forward, they regress backward in time to a place where they first came to this earth and need as much care as they did the day they were born. Dignity and love are the highest values needed and respected as someone journeys into the depths of Dementia. It is a grueling disease on loved ones and families that is certain, your knowledge level, understanding, compassion and attitude are the tools to keep your mind in the place where it is needed to be of support for your loved one.

It is and becomes a selfless road without recognition to the daily grind as Janice reflects moment to moment accounts and it impacts the whole family and your outer community as well.

As I watched each resident slipping away into this place that nobody, not even themselves could identify with, the confusion and fear was evident in their eyes and body language. For some this creates adverse reactions as the person fights out against general daily routines, even a shower or dressing can become an enormous feat. The truth is in their eyes, look deep enough they reach their soul for you to see, their fear arises as you venture near. All logic disappears and you, human entering their sphere is like a foreign object that suddenly appears.

You think this day was like yesterday and all routine disappears as fast as any memory whilst you, yourself hold back from the tears and of course your deepest fears. So today you find a new way to do things, a new way of listening, a new way of speaking, a new way of doing. All the while your loved one is shrinking, and you must be expanding at a rate you have never known before. You are evaluated, you are tried, and it is true you are exhausted, the only thing that feels like it exists is time.

While your fear can do this, they fear how can I do this. The control is lost on both sides. 'Control' the perceived ability we think we have until all control is surrendered to this disease. Vulnerability, safety, compassion, and love are all left up to trust, until eventually even that is lost.

When you read this book, the journey will become yours too, the rise and falls, the love, the hope, the despair, and the disbelief are all here on this journey thanks to Janice caring to share.

Forget Me Not – Janice and Barry –

Much love always, Sue Seaby

Diversional Therapist (Lifestyle Coordinator)

Coordinator Community Services

Manager Aged Care Community Services

Dementia Activity Training

Meeting the Challenges of Our Future Training

Brain Gym For Aged Care

Dementia Activity & Focus Training

Email shetime999@gmail.com

Website www.shetime.com.au

Chapter One

Where do I Begin...

What do you do when you have not even the slightest clue about the challenges besetting your partner?

What do you do when they are refusing to confide in you, either deliberately or inadvertently?

What step do you take to find out the truth from them about what is plaguing them when you witness some changes in their personality, even though they claim they are fine whenever you raise an eyebrow?

Imagine that you notice a new change in them. Imagine you observe that your loved ones are becoming a shadow of the human you used to know, yet you cannot put a name to what afflicts them. Imagine you discover they have paled over time in the absence of no logical explanation. Imagine that they withdraw from you every day, yet you cannot put your finger on the specifics of the situation.

Then one day you listen to your inner voice, and you quiz a little further seeking out what appears to be a simple answer; you witness that they do not know the answer to these simple questions. You observe as the element of frustration box them in, and they seem a bit confused, yet when you look at this same partner, you would say nothing was wrong. It seems so strange that a person's mind could fail on a simple question that the same person could quickly answer in their prime.

I was calm enough to examine the situation from a logical point of view as best I could. However, I struggled to answer the questions. Or at least, I struggled to do so with some element of accuracy. Mathematics was not my strong suit. Hence, it was understandable that I struggled with calculations at every turn. My daughter's studies were my major immediate challenge. Who would I turn to for help with her exercises? Would I get the right outcome for my daughter's homework?

I overheard my partner Barry and our daughter one time; he was helping her with her school assignment. I was torn apart by shock when I heard him tell her 4x7 equalled 32 when in fact they equalled 28.

At first, I tried not to think about it or read much meaning into his apparent oversight. However, I couldn't keep the scare to myself. When I spoke out almost rashly, my impulsion got the better of me.

"Since when did four times seven equal 32?" I inquired, raising an eyebrow. He was mute, so I continued. "What has happened to you solving multiplications? Aren't they a walkover for you any longer?"

I did not wait for his response before I hurried over to my daughter's side, peering down into her book for some answers that I could tell wouldn't be staring me back in the face. If he wouldn't give her the right answers, the least I could do as her parent was to rectify his mistake.

To think that Barry had always made easy work of Mathematics problems, regardless of how difficult any equation might have been for anyone in his age group. Alas, there he was seated, beside our daughter as if nothing had happened, unable to solve a multiplication question that even

I would answer with my eyes closed. A thousand and one thoughts raced in my heart as I wondered what could have gone wrong.

In that defining moment, I could not look him in the eyes. It was from shame. It was from fear that danced about in my eyes. Or it was just from utter confusion that rippled through my gut.

Even though the irony of that significant moment was not lost on me, I could not bring myself to do anything to comfort him. Heck, even I needed to be comforted. And there was the matter of our daughter and her assignment. I just decided on the best course of action: to salvage the mess.

I cleared my throat noiselessly as I dredged up a smile and stared in our daughter's direction. I must admit I felt for her – she looked a little puzzled herself. And being a precocious child that she was, always asking questions of everything even when the correct answer might stare her in the face, she dived for the multiplication booklet from her school bag. The booklet was one of the many gifts we had given her to celebrate her birthday.

"Dad, here it is. Here is the answer to four times seven," she said with excitement dancing in her eyes as she showed her father the right answer in the booklet, unwary of the tense atmosphere between her father and me.

Barry knew something was amiss too, that instant. He was quite frustrated; his brows furrowed. Being the calm person that he had always been, he shrugged and brushed the loud mistake off as if nothing had happened.

He turned to our daughter with a smile planking on his face, although his eyes admitted he had made a mistake. "Well, at least the book is right. So, follow it for all the multiplications sums that you must do."

We never revisited the issue. We left it hanging in the air, dangling, hanging over our heads like a sword of Damocles, one that might just spell doom for all of us if care was not taken swiftly. It was only a matter of time before the situation would take a turn for the worse. In the months that followed, we would soon discover that we had a path to walk, a journey unknown lay ahead of us. We would come to find out that our lives would be impacted by a development that Barry and I had barely given any modicum of attention. And for my daughter and myself, we would come to lose the best friend that both of us had ever known at that time.

For several days, I struggled inwardly with my latest discovery. It soon became a norm in the house, every school day. Our daughter would have to consult her booklet to solve a simple equation. On most occasions, our daughter would painfully spend more time doing her mathematics homework than she normally should. On other times, he would just hide under the pretext of being tired and refuse to help us, leaving both mother and daughter to slug it out between each other. On such occasions, he would sit and watch the TV, his eyes fixated on the screen. I did suspect he was not really focused on the images that reflected on the screen; it looked like it was the time for him to reflect and unburden himself of worries and frustration that might have piled up in him over a period.

Of a truth, I could not tell if he was watching the TV with contentment or was just staring at the screen, unobservantly. I could not tell whether he was content with anything. I recalled passing over his actions, thinking we all had our moments, and it was best I allowed him to have his. Unfortunately, I was quite insentient to different things about him. It soon dawned on me that my lack of observations would come back to haunt me; I would be lead on an unknown pathway in a bid to find out the truths that I had blinded my eyes to. I would watch my life change dramatically.

I might have ignored the disease if one of my loved ones had not fallen prey to its onslaught. Albeit I had little or no knowledge about Alzheimer's disease before Barry suffered it, I would come to learn in a hard way. It was a huge learning curve, one for which I was not prepared.

It all may sound a little confusing to believe. However, the point I am trying to make here is I did not know what was happening to my partner. In simpler terms: I was oblivious to what I was meant to know. His cognitive functions were being impaired, and I could not help lifting a finger to curb it in time. Heck, I was totally uninformed until I started witnessing different unignorable evidence in him. For what it is worth, I am glad that I had to face the unknown. If I had not, I would not have been prepared; I would not be as informed as I am now on the subject. Now, I have a better understanding of the power of the mind, especially its ability to perform.

Awareness Wisdom Awakeners

◇ Test and measure are a good awareness to have, record in a diary of events as they happen, it will show you evidence when needed.

◇ Be open to guidance coming to you, however, be specific to ask questions to really understand what you are dealing with.

◇ When you feel tension and feel like you are under attack in your mind, allow yourself to cry, allow yourself to go and stand on the grass and just ground yourself and take 5-10 minutes to breath. Breathe is good to calm you down.

◇ If the opportune avails for you find the waves of the ocean and set your feet into the sand and breath in with the wave coming in and allow the breath to work when the wave is going out. This will help you to feel balanced. Breath work helps to calm you.

Chapter Two

In the Beginning

When Barry and I met, back in 1975, I was as adventurous as they come. He was a tour coach driver, and I was a keen and willing passenger who was about to explore the vast spaces of Central Australia on a 16-day camping trip to Alice Springs and Ayres Rock.

Now that I think about it, I truly have not even the slightest idea why I had chosen the place for a holiday. Intuitively I had a knowing I was meant to go on this trip. At the time I did not understand what the impact of being intuitive meant as I do now.

All I remember was looking at the brochures in the travel shop of the local country town that I lived close too, wondering if I could really do it.

I felt a nudge from within me. "Of course, you can. Anything is possible you can go here and visit The Rock – a great lump of sandstone in the middle of the desert."

The weeks passed quickly, and I was registered and ready to take what would be a trip of a lifetime and the outset of a huge determinant in my life.

When I shared the news with my parents, they were not overly pleased with it. It was different from any holiday that I had embarked upon alongside the family. And then there I was about to board a coach for a place so far away from the family into the centre of Australia.

Dare I say that I had never experienced a camping holiday before. Yes, I was up for it. I wanted to do it and with anticipation I was able to board the 40-foot coach on a holiday of a lifetime. My parents were a little concerned. To them, it was quite risky to go on a trip with a group of people I did not know so they suggested I take a girlfriend from school to join me and explore the centre together.

Boarding this vessel was quite an experience in itself; it was a much larger bus (coach) than the ole school bus that often conveyed us to school. There were more seats and we even had to climb up three or four steps to be inside the coach. The curtains were a tartan colour, and the outside of the coach was maroon with Centralian Tours written down the side of it. I knew this because thanks to my father, I knew the number plate of the bus before it took off, so I knew what coach I was on as a way of identifying and finding the right bus when travelling. The tartan curtains were unique as well. It was in-grained in my memory, and it did not take long before I understood how coach stations worked.

We were off as the coach kicked into life from the pavement. It was all packed in. There was nothing left on the pavement because our trip had just begun. I was excited to be a part of the trip. And in the buzz, I joined people greeting one another over the top of their seats and to the sides as best we could.

Nobody knew anyone else except for the families that were travelling together and the friends that were buddied up together. Of the thirty-eight people on board, eleven of those were kids under twelve; nine of us were under twenty-five and the balance of eighteen were over twenty-five. It was safe to assume that it was a compact group of people. From memory we had one lady over fifty-five and the rest were an average age of thirty-five. We had three representatives from the company who were the Courier – Mike and Wendy the Cook and Barry the Driver. While Barry shared statistics and provided general information on the rules and guidelines on the trip, Mike and Wendy shared the mic on separate occasions for the first part of the journey. It was all extremely exciting; our first stop was Mildura for lunch.

It was here at Mildura that my life felt a small impact, the Driver came over to the group of under twenty-five's who were all standing around, getting to know each other when he politely asked who could make coffee.

I was so quick to get my hand up only to be nominated as the coffee maker for the rest of the trip. Little did I know I would be making the coffee for years later as well! White, with two sugars was the request and so I made the coffee morning afternoon and night sometimes with rum in it at night-time, for all the sixteen camping days that we were away.

The trip was exciting, and we explored Australia's outlying country that the average Australian may never get to see. It was a place called William Creek, red dust dirt and large numbers of flies and open spaces yet a small place on the map was one of the day's lunch breaks. If I had not gone on the trip, my eyes might not have been open to the sparse open spaces of the Australian country.

There were no lush green hills only flat dry creek beds and open plains very scarce of grasses for the animals to eat. There were no animals to see either: we came across a couple however they were lying dead on the side of the roads, either hit by other vehicles or had starved to death. I had come from a lush verdant farming area, so it was a bit of a shock to witness such harsh dry grounds.

Before we could as much as blink, the sixteen days were over; the reality of going back to our previous lives stared us in the face. We knew we had to pick up from where we had left off before the journey. The swing of life awaited us. My best takeaway from the journey had been meeting Barry. He and I had bonded during the trip. It was not difficult for us to stay in contact on our return journey to Melbourne.

Upon our return from the trip, I took a permanent leave of my job in the local country, relocating instead to the city where I worked in a cake factory. Barry was quite fortunate though: upon his return as well, he was offered another job, one that was best suited to his skills. The end of the trip meant that Barry was out of work. The owner of the coach had an open spot for a mechanic. He did not hesitate to take it up. He could turn his hands to better use, from having to drive people around on their journeys, he could repair the coaches they rode in. It was quite easier for him since he felt at home on the job.

The cold of Melbourne was a bit too much for Barry and he longed for the warmer weather back in Darwin. The only reason he was in Melbourne was he was taking time from Darwin from witnessing Cyclone Tracy. It was here he was in the coach industry as well.

I had been unemployed on two separate occasions myself and it did not take long before I began to discuss a relocation to Darwin with him. Since he was open to the suggestion, I chose to travel with him, so off we went.

With Barry being an astute mechanic, the owner of the coach we travelled on also was the owner of a Ferry in Darwin. With Barry's return to Darwin the Ferry owner needed to get a motor for the said ferry into Darwin and this become the logical purpose for us to travel. Barry had worked on the motor for the ferry, so it was not difficult for him to convey this unit with Barry's return. The trip to Darwin, became a necessity and it allowed him work in Darwin as a starter.

Meanwhile, I had not decided on what I intended to do with my life. There was no job in sight in Melbourne. There was no active plan in the works. All I knew was that I wanted a change of scenery, the rest would sort itself out. Saddled with the likelihood that I might hate the place in the space of weeks or months because the weather might just be too hot to be inhabitable for me, I left Melbourne with Barry and set up in Darwin, we had towed a caravan with us, so we had a roof over our heads. I could not be more surprised to find out I loved it. With Barry beside me, this was to be our home for an around 10 years.

As the years rolled on, we both had work in the Public Service, and we had bought a larger caravan to live in. It was quite small: it was just forty-foot long and nine feet wide. We had to tow it from Melbourne to Darwin. Life was good. Together, we enjoyed barramundi fishing, and we spent nights camping under the stars.

In 1982 when our daughter arrived, life happens, and things changed. This spurred us into reviewing our lives to accommodate the third member of our little family. That meant we had to add an extension to the van like an annexe. When I was heavily pregnant, I had to stay off work and things remained like that until our daughter was five months old. The office asked if I could return to work, and my leave was close to finished. Things were quite difficult living on just Barry's salary for six good months. It was quite draining to live off his salary and things were quite tight. Once our daughter was five months, I returned to work.

Despite the busy schedules, we still tried to enjoy the camping and fishing now and then. The only difference was that it was no longer on weekends like we used to have all to ourselves.

We resorted to one-day events and short stay overnighters. It was a great lifestyle. We also grew to love the elusive Orchid after a trip to Singapore in 1985.

Later in 1985 I was to witness my first experiences of dealing with life's challenges as it happened at that time, our local fire brigade to which Barry was a member was first to attend a local out of control fire in the open woodlands in our area.

Barry was caught in the fire; trust me it was not a pretty sight to see. He suffered burns on the upper part of his body and third-degree burns to the back of his hands. Visiting the hospital every day and watching the nurses lift the slurry as they called it from Barry's arms and hands was one of the hardest things to deal with at that point in life. I could not plan to be there when they were attending to him. At first, it was just at random, they would do this as it took hours to unwrap and then to spend the time on each piece of skin lifting from the body. Credit to the nurses, it was not something I was able to stomach all the time. On most occasions, I nearly drowned in tears watching him groan in pain. It was not the easiest of situations to witness especially when you saw that your partner was in pain.

Our lives moved forward and after the body had healed itself, we took a long trip south to revisit our plans, and of course, life's direction. We had it in mind that we might leave Darwin at a point in time. However, what we were to witness was to be an advantage having travelled for a couple of weeks.

We had to be at our best to be understanding of each other's differences at that time. And as one does face challenges in one's everyday life, including a throng of highs and lows, our family would soon be hit with a scary health issue that afflicted my partner. His good heart left him quite unsteady. He was obviously concerned for the well-being of his family, especially if his health might take a turn for the worse. Our trip away from home did help lift our spirits with his health scare of the healing of the fire incident.

During those past seven years, Barry had developed signs of head nodding and shaking. And although it was not overly noticeable all the time, it was there, and it started to exacerbate as each day went by. After numerous visits to the doctors, he was given medication indicating that he had a mild strain of Parkinson disease. Sinemet tablets, did help ease the shaking and wobbling. We must have thought he was out of the woods with that for we never really thought much of it after he had been prescribed drugs by a doctor.

The only serious concerns that we had were about his ability to drive and his tendency to function at an optimal level around the house should it slip his mind to take his drugs. It was again a hard thing to watch and without the technology that we have today, research was not as easy as it is now, then on the internet. Hence, often, one had to be guided by the doctor's point of view. I witnessed a lot of movement and sharp jolts in the body throughout the night's sleep; yet Barry had no idea it was happening. He never felt any discomfort. For me it was hard to watch at times. He would be sitting in the chair, and he was nodding yet he did not feel the effect of this. He was a very strong-willed man and I just had to watch as each step of his life unfolded with his age.

Perhaps I left out a very important part of our journey. I should apologise. Well, I don't know if it does count though, Barry was twenty-two years older than I was. And in the space of ten years of love, we had a lovely daughter who was almost five when we left the Territory. She was born in the Territory and had completed her primary years of school in Mackay.

Our family was made up of 3 generations: Barry was born in the 30's I was born in the 50's and our daughter was in the 80's. Barry and I met in the '70s, and we gave birth to our daughter in '82. So, it was safe to note that we had a unique family indeed. Our lives had been very happy whilst living in Mackay however Barry's health had started to show telling signs on his age. The seeming diagnosis of a mild strain of Parkinson Disease wasn't helping our situation either.

The next noticeable thing that my daughter and I witnessed was that Barry was losing some of his concentration on things. One minute, he was misplacing the car keys or some other random object that he had left on some surface. Another time, he might not have a recollection of what he was looking for in the first place.

One could have argued that it came with age however it became very evident in many things like personal information. For instance, information about where we lived, phone numbers, things in everyday life became more and more elusive to him. He could barely remember all these basic pieces of information.

Our daughter also recalled times when Barry held the position as president of the club we belonged to and sometimes he forgot where he was up in the middle of a conversation. He used to laugh it off at the time though, refusing to let it get to him. He was a very sharp-witted man and had a huge knowledge base especially from all the travelling in the tourist industry he had done.

We were living with his condition every day and really didn't notice it a lot only the days when he forgot to take his medication. Whilst on the medication he managed everything quite all right. I really didn't worry about it; we just moved on with life normally, like nothing was happening. In Barry's past he had been involved in a few fights that I had known him and had a few head butts to the forehead however never really complaining of pain or suffering so nothing was ever recorded. He had a fair share of smoking during his hay days, be it the odd piece of marijuana or some other heavier drugs. No one could blame him: it was the era he had grown up in. He would share some stories with me during the early days and he soon realised it was not something I wanted to deal with nor was I happy about. He had completed those days when I met him. Now as true as you are reading this story my intuition told me something at the time however, I was not in tune with it as flashing thoughts would cross my mind, I wondered if he will ever have any side effects in his life. It was gone as fast as it came so I never really understood why I had those thoughts. I just did. I was doing things and played in life to the best of my ability, those thoughts were for old people not for me and so life just moved on.

I never really gave it a lot of attention.

*** **** ***

An opportune moment soon came for us. We had to take a trip back to Darwin, to attend an Australian Orchid Conference.

This trip to Darwin had us both excited – one, we both had left the Territory with a feeling that we might get to return one day however, within us, Barry's redundancy had left us with a bittersweet taste of leaving for good. So, it was good to know what this pending trip would do for us both.

Would we have a pull to return to Darwin or would we recognise that we had made the right decisions and stay in Mackay? As they say the World is your Oyster and we were about to find out the truth.

We were going back to Darwin.

Our trip back to Darwin for the Orchid conference 1994 was a huge turning point for Barry and me, especially after we had spent seven years in Mackay. On this journey, we had numerous conversations, and at times my partner was a little vague with some conversations, I just never picked up on the specifics, just accepted what transpired between us as part of life. I was none the wiser at the time. Our time in Darwin triggered an inexplicable feeling in us that spurred us into wanting to return to Darwin. The travel back to Mackay was confirmed however as we drove closer to our Qld property; we both knew we did not want to return to Mackay. We still had an hour's drive to go when our conversation really become very constructive. We were just on the south side of Proserpine heading towards Mackay when we struck a conversation that would change our lives again.

The closer we drove to the Mackay property, the more reserved we both became in returning to Mackay. Something had wanted us both to want to return to Darwin, something had stirred the old emotions in us alive, seeking us to choose Darwin over Mackay.

We kept questioning the reason while trying to work out what was making us feel this way. For most of the journey back home, we were quiet. And we had already driven 3000 kilometres away from Darwin, with barely twenty minutes to go from the Mackay home at Habana, when we turned to each other almost concurrently: "Let's sell up and go back". We looked at each other and smiled. In that defining moment, something felt right and our whole perspective on things changed.

There was no going back. We had decided on returning to Darwin, the place where our lives together had practically begun. Of a truth, neither of us felt at peace driving back to the property in Mackay as we had felt back in Darwin when we left seven years earlier.

Awareness Wisdom Awakeners

◇ Always play a game around where you live as an awareness of memory and the awareness around those areas of information to be a good indicator it keeps you alert.

◇ Sometimes change can impact our lifestyles – be grateful.

◇ Your intuition is always guiding you to do what is needed to be done on this journey. Trust and believe it will show you a way.

◇ Understand you are following your heart when it feels good to take that next step. Come the resolution in making that decision. When you are comfortable with the plans you are making and no obstructions from your gut then you are in flow, and everything is making progress for the next outcome. Trust yourself it will be right.

Chapter Three

Lost on the Property

It was an eerie feeling, yet it also felt right when, after barely what took moments, I noticed my partner picking up his small habits of forgetfulness. I just let things slide, deliberately choosing to ignore rather than dwell on it. Roaming the property was one of them, never knowing why he was there.

Our arrival back at the Mackay home had us both feeling quite uneasy, yet we knew we had to return to work and get back into the swing of things. We started to look at a business in Darwin as a way of going back to something we could work together in rather than finding a job, this moved quickly on some levels and at one point we had a lot of interest in the market for our house, it was at this turning point that we had found a venue to look at in Darwin and so Barry boarded a plane to inspect the property and to check out the viability of the business. To date I don't recall the specifics of what happened, however, I do believe that the figures were good, and the locality was in a booming commercial area. The cause was that Barry was not able to clearly see his way with the figures for the growth of the business. The owner of the business called me to say they were witnessing Barry not comprehending everything and this caused for things to come to a halt. So, we no longer had any interest in the property. When the owner of the business rings you and shares that the partner is not absorbing everything, you must sit and ponder on what is being said, sadly I think I didn't want to hear anything as I had not accepted what was happening to be real for us and life just kept moving on. It was hard to hear these words yet no real evidence in front of you.

For us it was a big letdown on something that had looked quite promising. In hindsight, when I think back now maybe it was a good move. Perhaps, the market had to suffer that level of setback for our sake or for all the right reasons. I wasn't as interested in it as my partner had been at the time. It didn't resonate with me for some unknown reason, maybe it was a sign I did not want to go down that path, however it was what it was, and we carried on regardless. So, the letdown didn't get to me as it might have got to him. Barry seemed to drop his bundle as well and we just plodded on as normal people would do with a hope that by Christmas we could be sold. Also, we changed our real estate after the primary exclusive time was up and moved to a more rural market agent.

Our daughter was around 12 years of age when we decided to return to Darwin, so it was considered that finishing her primary years in Qld was good, the next move was to find her a conducive high school. Having travelled to Darwin in the middle of the year, the discussion about the Northern Territory local high schools really didn't cross our minds. It wasn't until we had made our decision that our daughter would change schools and move to Darwin for her high school years that we acted on our plans for her. She did not have much say in this matter, we had friends at Darwin High so we worked on getting our daughter to stay with them until we could move ourselves.

The plan was to see our daughter get through her junior school, which was her final year at primary school. Hence, the timing was also right for us to move again. Having travelled to Darwin in July we still had several months to get things organised. We had a house to tidy up and get a lick and a promise of spring clean and overall get our property on the market as quick as we could. We had been at the same property for seven years.

That meant a lot of work had to be done to get the house back in good conditions and a good clean and polish up.

For instance, it needed to be cleaned and patched up here and there; the windows needed a little hammering in, and most parts of the house required a repainting. The garden had to be tidied up and put into order for open house inspections. We gave the house a spring cleaning, reached the real estate requirements and were ready to put the house on the market within a 6-week period. At that time the market was a bit unstable, and pricing was average for sales of homes in the outer areas of Mackay. We kept the house price within the recommended market value because we were hoping for a quick sale. I was left to do all of this and to get things organised maybe because that is what I do best. Even though I did what I did to the best of my abilities, I often wonder whether it was easier because Barry did not have to get involved.

There is never a good time to sell a house, most times you must go with the market flow and wait for a buyer to step forward. Around this time, Barry started getting a little bit distracted and distant. I did not think much of it at the time and attributed his change in behaviour to the stress that comes with moving and the uncertainty as to what comes next. I understood that at the age of fifty-nine it was a huge uplift for any man to leave behind a place he was adjusted to for so many years. However, on one or two occasions I found him wandering the five-acre block with no sense of direction and no reason to be where he was at that point in time.

Our property was on a hill with a reasonable acclivity to the summit. The house was sitting on a flat piece of land that had been carved out of the hill, so it overlooked the lower part of the block and creek that ran the length of the property on the western side. Occasionally, I caught him dawdling with our dog in the grass at the edge of the creek. This would draw my attention and make me wonder what he was doing, because there was no reason for him to be on the property at that point in time. One afternoon, I grew curious enough to walk down to the creek to see what he was doing. When we first moved into the property, we had planted over three hundred trees; however, we lost eighty percent of them due to heavy and constant rainfall. One night it rained twenty-six inches during a 24-hour period. However, Barry was not looking at the plants, he was walking slowly towards the edge of the creek. I called to him, and yet, he did not respond; I was confused because the dog heard me and looked towards my direction, alas, Barry was lost in a world of his own. It was not till I was close to him that he jumped at my presence as though he had not seen or heard me arrive. I must admit that at that point in time I thought of his behaviors as very odd, because we had a close and open relationship. We shared with each other wherever we were going to on the property; there were several Taipans around the creek, because of the sugarcanes planted there, there were also pockets of water in the creek, so the appearance of a snake was inevitable. It was so unusual for him not to respond and then be startled by my presence. At the time I did not know that it was the beginning of something that would be heart-wrenching to witness.

The second and third time it happened; he was walking along the path of the driveway in front of the house. I called him again only to be ignored, I noticed that he seemed so far away, like he was in a different land. It was not unusual for him to be so lost in his thoughts. There was something different about him these past few months. I thought something must have gone wrong somewhere, and yet I did nothing about it. By the time I reached Barry, he was in a daze, he looked so disoriented saying.

"I was doing something, and I just cannot think of what I was going to do"

I replied, "well, where were you last, and go back there".

He had an idea as to where he was, and he was not working at the front of the property he was at the back of the property. He said he could not remember so I walked with him to the 3-bay shed because it was a good starting point, we could see just about all the property from that point. I recall asking some questions, like

"Okay what direction did you come from?"

"I think it was that way", he pointed towards the back, which to me was correct considering that he was at the back of the property where our shade houses were.

"What did you come to the shed to do?"

"I don't remember" he said, hmm I thought, as I had noticed that he had a long screwdriver in his back pocket, so I asked

"Was it for the screwdriver?"

"Ahh, I remember it was because I needed to get another item to work on in the shade house at the back," said Barry. He picked up a clamp and more tools.

"Okay," I said, we then proceeded to walk through the narrow pathway that led to the large orchid shade houses at the back of the property, he was completing some watering systems for the plants to get water overhead rather than doing it by hand. He had set up timers, so it was all automated with a fine mist. Barry had momentarily lost his cognitive function as I think back now, whilst I write. I witnessed this off and on for several months, nothing really seemed to change he seemed happy and like he was just getting back into shape.

I had no idea what was happening at that point in time internally for him. He never shared anything with me, so I was none the wiser of what was happening. He began to tinker with the pipes and fittings, and I proceeded to walk back to the house after losing 30 minutes of my time. I muttered to myself saying

'What a silly old fool, surely he can't have Alzheimer's at such a young age'.

I was to be proven wrong. I did not think much of it however at the time it crossed my mind on several occasions what was happening to him and what if Alzheimer's would be the outcome of his forgetfulness. I had not really given it a lot of attention only fleeting moments of this thought ever crossed my mind. I just continued with what I was doing at the time.

Life moved on and Barry was assessed by his doctor and specialist on 6 monthly intervals and there did not seem to be any real decline in his health, so we plodded on our merry way. His shaking of head and limbs seemed to be under control due to the tablets he was taking, and the medication overall left him with a relatively steady hand. We both knew the days he had forgotten to take his medication because his hand movements and head would show evidence.

As much as Barry said he had not forgotten, it was the convincing tone of his daughter's words that would have him take the medication. She seemed to just reach him in a way that I did not. It did not bother me though, at least he was listening to her.

Now if I could make any other comments to the progress of Barry around this time was that whilst I was preparing tea most evenings Barry would sit with our daughter and do her homework at the kitchen table. On some occasions I noticed that he was not adding up correctly and the answers to the mathematics that the daughter had for homework were coming out all wrong.

Some of those tricky multiplications that always used to come easy to him had begun to confuse Barry and it was on one occasion that we had bought an addition, subtraction, and multiplication book for our daughter that she tested dad as they did the homework. One may think I should have seen something here at this point, however when it is a close love you don't always see everything occurring and I was still in denial of such an event would be taking place.

I noticed, with some concern, that one day Barry left the table a little distressed. He could no longer be around the numbers, and he proceeded to watch TV. I helped our daughter with her math equations and never spoke of it again with Barry. I was just careful to observe the questions of the mathematics homework our daughter had so that it did not upset or confuse Barry. I had no idea how much pain he might have been in now, neither did I understand what was happening. I never confronted him in front of our daughter, and by the time I mentioned some of the things I was talking about he would have forgotten; so, I never pushed the subject.

Awareness Wisdom Awakeners

◇ Mathematics is basically in the central part of the brain and one of the first area's we witnessed for non-functionality for Barry. Doing a small easy test of mathematics can be an indication to your situation.

◇ The hardest part is to be able to tie all the indicators to a result, not all will show themselves clearly and not everyone is the same.

◇ Forgetfulness is something that occurs at any age, however when the same questions or statements are asked repeatedly, then you may have more on your hands to deal with.

◇ Look at it gently and seek some guidance from your doctor first. Then arrange for the respective steps to take place. This is not a rush it is a journey, and you have a family member to always remember and attend to as well.

Chapter Four

We need a New Trailer - 'What?

Things moved along their merry way and finally after about 5-6 months our property was to be sold.

This really had us shift into a new gear as we really started to put together a clearing sale of all surplus items we had. We had to pull down and sell orchid houses of which there were 3 large ones and all the stock inside as little by little we closed the nursery side of operations down.

Moving back to Darwin we only took plants that were special to us; about 24 it was also a time to move on from this chapter of our life as that was closing. With the Orchid Nursery officially closed, all plants had sold along with the shade houses; we were getting closer to leaving the property.

In the interim period before we closed the Nursery we had taken on the selling of plastic garden pots at the local market and this also had an opportunity for us to sell the pots individually or as a complete bulk and it occurred on one day that a lady offered to buy the lot as a bulk deal, she wanted to continue the sales as she had noticed we had done rather well from all the sales.

What I witnessed during this time was quite amazing as Barry left all the transactions up to me to deal with and all the finances were left in my hands to sort out. All Barry wanted to do was get the pots out of the house and into the other person's car.

He had started to do this prior to confirmation that the sale was completed. I was so startled by this action, and a bit annoyed. However, it all happened so fast that we all made a joke of it, and I never followed through as to why he did it. Maybe as I type now, I realize that it was a sign of cognitive functions starting to fail him, and I had no idea what it was or why it was happening.

With the sale of garden pots to which I might add was about 800 pots that took place, we made a reasonable profit from the complete sale done. I organised for a clearing sale day at the property, and it wasn't long before all the sellable items were gone, and we could really feel that moving was a reality.

Barry was a little confused from it all as at one point several sales were all being completed for the same item and I had to come to help Barry sort it out, because he looked so overwhelmed with confusion. There was some heavy bartering for our TE20 Fergie Tractor, it was a hit among the local small farmers. We bought it for just $2000 and we sold it $200 over $2000 so we were happy by the end of the sale.

With all saleable items removed from the property, all that was left were our personal effects to be packed into our 7x4 trailer. Our suitcases were ready, and the house items removed we only had to pack our camping items and we were ready to leave. It became really evident to me on this day that there was something even more noticeably wrong with Barry.

Barry had packed this trailer several times, so it was nothing new. However, what happened that day convinced me that there was something going on with him more than I understood. Our trailer was designed by Barry and built for specific camping items enabling everything to fit in snuggly and load evenly in the trailer. We added a cage for our dog to travel in, within the Trailer area.

This part of the story shares when I really became aware that something was not right with Barry. Barry had designed the trailer when we first bought it; he had drawn it all to scale at the time so that everything we wanted to fit in there was either placed inside a compartmented box or a box that fit perfectly in the trailer very tightly. I was totally alarmed when Barry come into the house on the final day saying we are going to have to get another trailer as nothing was fitting into the space or that we would have to leave the dog behind because her cage would not fit. I was extremely shocked at what he said.

"What do you mean? it has always fitted before, so why doesn't it fit now that we have no more than what we pack for camping?"

I was probably ranting currently, and I was exhausted, packing up was a huge job. We had sent our daughter ahead of us to Darwin because school was about to begin and we wanted her to be there for the beginning of the term, so we arranged for her to stay with some of our friends. Barry and I would be on our way as soon as the solicitor cleared the money.

I went out to the shed and looked at the trailer and was amazed at all the stuff Barry had left on the ground. Our belongings were not tightly packed into the trailer, he had only turned everything around, things were not in the right place. The boxes that were supposed to be at the shorter side of the trailer were at the longer side and vice versa, if he had packed it the other way around, there would have been more room.

The trailer had been designed in a way that everything would fit perfectly, and it was evident that this had not been done.

I started moving the boxes to their proper place, I called for things and Barry handed them to me.

The dog a basset hound had been left sitting in her cage, so she was not going anywhere. The amazing thing about this was Barry used to pack coaches and could fit large numbers of cases into tight spots, so this was so out of character. Something was wrong somewhere and I just could not put my finger on it.

Fifteen to twenty minutes later, it was evident that everything was going to fit, and Barry stood there scratching his head saying, "I couldn't see how it was going to fit so that's why I called you."

He couldn't make out what he had done, we lifted the dog in its cage into the back of the last space on the trailer and proceeded to close the gate, as everything was in, dog and all. I recall going back to the house and feeling overwhelmed at what happened, I even shed a tear, the finale was close, all we waited for now was the phone call from the Solicitor.

As I sit here, typing, I can see that day unfolding quite clearly in my mind, I was just not attuned to what was happening to Barry to really understand the suffering or confusion (if any) he was going through. For all I knew, he was a silly old man and had forgotten how to pack his trailer, this was a thought I never voiced these words just kept to myself.

I just kept moving forward, what was in store was about to unveil itself; it was all just a matter of real time to see and witness the change in the man and there was nothing I could do to assist or make it better. His body was showing signs of cognitive functionality waning and it was just a matter of time as each signal exposed itself to us.

Awareness Wisdom Awakeners

◇ Being mindful of small changes could be your biggest indicator, if they were happening a lot of times.

◇ The minds capacity is huge and being clear on instruction can also lead to hearing and understanding.

◇ Repetitions on something said is annoying to the receiver however a good indication something is not quite right.

◇ Upheaval can cause confusion to the recipient make smaller changes over time.

◇ Being mindful that moments of looking lost could be associated to comprehension of where the person is at. A little lost no real idea why they are where they are or looking for something yet not knowing why they are looking.

Chapter Five

Sorting Wills and Contract

Our drive to Darwin also brought a few things to my attention, once or twice we were heading for the bush as Barry become dazed whilst driving and I had to make sure he was alert and touch him on the arm or ask him a question to be sure that he was concentrating.

I become more aware and did not sleep as much in the car during the journey up to Darwin. I drove a lot more as well. I just felt the necessity to take control for want of a better word. I wanted to arrive safe and sound and to see our daughter again and be together once more as a family, this whole experience had really opened our family up and to be separated for a short period of time.

When we arrived safely in Darwin, the first thing we did was reconnect with our daughter and find suitable accommodations. Luckily, we found accommodation quickly and we could at least settle for some time.

We also started to look for businesses that were for sale, because this was the best way to generate income at the time. The Mackay house sale had left us with a reasonable amount to live off; however, it was not going to last a lifetime and with a medium sized portion to buy a business it wasn't long before the money was moving faster than we had envisaged. A decision had to be made regarding the 15-seater bus we drove to Darwin; do we repair or find a more suitable car.

We had been avid fans of Mazda during our previous years in Darwin, so we ventured to the Mazda yard. The first car we looked at with interest was the vehicle we drove out of the yard. As luck would have it, I was able to get a good deal on a demo car; the last of the stock and bartered with the rep to take our car as a trade in on the demo model, I also knocked another $2000 from the sale price, and we drove away with a brand-new demo "Bravo" Ute model. It already had around 15000km on the clock, so the first service was done all we needed to do was put a canopy on the back and we were back in business to go fishing and camping again. We were extremely happy with our purchases; I was certain we got a good deal.

At the time it all seemed like the right thing to do. Now as fate would have it, and during the journey back to Darwin about getting our wills in order, what an insight this proved to be as life had a message to share and it was about to be obvious what this was as time proceeded. The solicitor also become our legal consult for signing our business details and we also signed our wills and power of attorney at the same time. Those days there was no indication of anything wrong with comprehension because Barry was able to read what had to be read when we signed all documents. Life was moving forward to the best of my knowledge.

At the solicitor meeting, it became very evident to our daughter that her dad had other children from a previous relationship. Even though Barry chose not to share this with his daughter at the time it did become a god send for her to find out during this meeting. As the days went on, our daughter would have a duty to contact the former next of kin to share the news of their dad as things unfolded. A very big task for a young girl such as herself to have to fulfil.

With the signing of our wills and power of Attorney out of the way, then next we proceeded to iron out the details for the shop we were about to purchase, a purchase that would impact our lives in more ways than one.

During the handover process of our newly purchased business, it became more evident that that there was something going on with Barry. It was the stress of the shop purchase that had an impact on him in many ways.

Having just arrived at Darwin in the past month or so, we had not found a new specialist doctor to get Barry accessed. We had with us a letter to share from our doctor in Mackay, we just had not made the appointments yet. We just started the first week of our new trade, at this point, things always went smoothly while we were learning the new processes; and this was not the case for the both of us.

It became very evident when the past owner, Evan who was training Barry first called me into the shop and said I needed to do something, because Barry appeared to not be listening to anything he was saying. He complained that Barry also seemed absent minded, he was not comprehending any of his instructions. I looked at Evan at the time and asked, "Are you sure"?

Something inside my gut sank into a deep hole. 'What had we done?' I asked myself. I felt numb from the words I had just heard, hearing it come from someone else was like third party credibility, I just was not ready to take the words to heart, I could comprehend what was being said to me. We were committed to keep this shop alive and going and it was only our first week. I felt such a strain on my shoulders, an unknown ache developed deep inside me, what had I done to our family?

I asked myself because that was all of which I could think. Evan had been a gentleman when he was sharing what he had witnessed, his message was so strong, he sounded concerned, saying that I needed to learn all the aspects of the shop. He told me that even after he repeated the same information repeatedly, Barry just did not seem to be getting it. I looked at Evan, still startled from the onslaught of information.

"What do you mean?" I asked. He told me that the hand over will be finished in three days and Barry still was not absorbing or comprehending what he was trying to teach. It took me a couple of days to snap out of the numbness I felt after hearing what Evan said. I knew I had to pull myself together because I had to make the business work out, for my family. I was depending on Barry to pull his way through and do what needed to be done to make this work.

I must have sounded shocked when I replied, "Oh I see... umm ok well, I will be here tomorrow, and we can go from there".

Again, my heart sank, 'what could be wrong with Barry?' I thought, what could be happening, maybe this guy is seeing things from a different angle because he is not sure how Barry operates. Barry had been a tour coach driver and he had cooked for several people on a large BBQ. This was no different, even though it was indoors and on just as large a plate as the outdoor BBQ.

I always got our daughter ready for school and dropped her off, then I would go to the shop around 8am. The new development made me turn things around, I had to be at the shop first while Barry dropped our daughter off at school. I had her keep an eye on him to make sure that he was ready to go at the right time. Even though this worked for a while, it became evident that it was best for all of us to leave at the same time. From the shop, our daughter could walk to school since it was not a long walk. It was a small take away food shop that we decided to name 'Tucka Hut', we cooked eggs, and bacon sandwiches, hot pies, and other types of pastries. We would leave home at 5am so that we could get to the shop by 6am to get things set up and prepare for our first customer by around 7am.

There were always smoko orders on the phone that come through around 7.30, they had to be prepared and delivered around 9.30am, so we were always busy from the moment we stepped into the shop till the early hours of the afternoon. After taking over the ownership of the business, it became increasingly obvious that the process of cooking and making sandwiches for customers was hard for Barry. He couldn't remember all the ingredients of a salad and a bacon sandwich. He got lost one morning while making a delivery; he told me that he went to the wrong place because he couldn't remember the name of the shop he was supposed to go to. Barry was assigned the role of the chief cook and he seemed to handle this well up until the moment he lost an egg and bacon roll one morning and he never seemed to be able to carry out the orders simply anymore. Another staff member had to assist to make sure everything was being done right. We all had a role to perform, Tracey and the other staff members did not mind assisting him. When Tracey left, we noticed some changes in Barry, they were small yet significant to the development of his ability. By now, I had reconnected with our old Doctor, and he was happy to share with us, the contact of a Neurosurgeon who visited Darwin from Cairns every 3-6 months, it wasn't long before Barry was able to get re assessed.

The fact that he was still on the tablets and seemed like he was barely coping raised a new level of concern, even though it was still his early days. I think the final straw was on the day we all forgot to set the food warmer on and by the time it had to be delivered, it was partly cold, and not preheated in the warmer. This had a negative impact on our sales; we even got some abusive phone calls from customers that were not happy. Even though this was not Barry's fault, it was obvious that he did not check the temperature of the food warmer as he put the food in while I was busy serving the customers that were coming in at the counter at a steady flow.

On the days prior to the food warmer incident, Barry had ended up at a wrong place to deliver food and he had no idea where he was. The owner of that shop called to say that they did not order food and Barry was at their shop, unsure of where he had to go. This had a negative impact on our sales as well, and it was starting to become evident that one of us had to make a change, because if this continued, it would be disastrous. I decided to send one of the staff out while I managed the shop. We had only been in the business no more than 4 months, and we had a 12-month lease, I knew then that it was going to be a long year. Sales were starting to deplete, and we were struggling to make ends meet, something had to change.

It was evident that Barry had to go out and get some work. I thought about this for several days and thought that perhaps it was best for him to go back to his line of work in the mechanical industry. It must have been such a huge change for him to be in the shop all day when he was used to a more exciting life. I had come this far on my own, surely it could not get any harder. I calculated because my daughter was there to help in the mornings, and she would come back in by noon, I would hire staff for the rest of the day to get through.

So, with some understanding of what was happening, yet no real comprehension about what was really going on with Barry, I approached him to discuss the possibility for him going to the job centre and trying to find some work. He seemed to be in the right frame of mind and said it would be hard to do because he was much older now. I left it at that for a couple more days until I was able to encourage him to take that next step.

I still hang on to the idea that everyone makes mistakes, and it was evident that not everything was clear for me to see nor understand what was happening for Barry. I was trying my hardest to stay afloat for myself let alone understand with empathy what was not working for Barry.

I was carrying a huge burden, and my own level of stress was enough; making the rent for the shop keeping the till filled with money to pay for the goods and services that were needed to keep the shop afloat. By the end of the financial year, we had nearly exhausted all our savings and things were not as good as I had hoped. I was able to manage the shop for about another 3 months when the decision was made that it was time to break the lease and get out. I had come to the end of my tether, and I was really starting to see different sides of Barry repeating more often than I had seen in the previous months. It was all starting to come together; however, the proof was still to be confirmed I was merely working on what I was witnessing. Our daughter had also noticed that during her conversations with her dad, he would often ask the same questions several times. This always affected the both of us because on other days, he seemed fine, so it was hard to determine the symptoms.

Buying a small takeaway shop ended up being one of the biggest mistakes we could have made. Despite having comprehensive discussions with the owner at the time and gaining advice from the small business enterprise department; as it was known, we proceeded to buy this small take away business. We were both so inexperienced in this field that it let us both down. As the months rolled on, we had lots of staff and at one point we barely brought in enough money for the rent let alone for us to live our private lives. My partner just kept plodding on and doing his best in the shop. I knew he was not enjoying this journey neither was I. By the 6- or 7-month things had begun changing once again. I could see that the new business was making my partner very stressed, and it had come to a crunch when I suggested that Barry go out and get a job. This time he took my suggestion with a smile; his mood seemed to pick up. Unfortunately, he did not get a job after three weeks; I found this weird because he had held supervisory positions in the past. Still, I remained supportive and encouraged Barry to look for another job.

Barry got fired a few weeks into his second job. He came back to the shop, looking disappointed; he sat down and wept, telling me that there were no more jobs for him. This was the second time he got fired in a short number of months since he started job hunting. He told me that he lost his way, and that was why he was fired from his second job. I did something I wouldn't normally do; I went to my husband's former workplace to speak with the owner. I called him first to be sure if he was okay with me coming to see him. When I arrived at the business, he was on the phone, and I waited outside the mechanical premise until he had finished his business on the phone. I was dressed in the white t-shirt and apron because I had made the decision to go on the spot.

I wanted to find out why Barry had been sacked within just a few short weeks of employment. I was offered a chair in the office that was full of grease and black markings, I endeavoured to stay off the arms of the chair and sat on only a short piece of the base, the chair was quite dirty. The owner of Barry's previous workplace was a Dutchman, he seemed very nice. During our conversation, it was obvious that he did not know where to start. He knew I was there searching for some answers about Barry's employment.

"I think your husband is ill," he said.

"Oh" I said, a little surprised. "What makes you say that?" I asked, leaning forward.

Don went on to say that at first, the boys in the workshop were tolerant of the questions Barry kept asking; however, after the first week, they started to grow tired of the same questions and repeating everything often. Barry was not comprehending what was being said to him, he said that he could not work with a man who can't work with instructions. I looked at him, shocked at what I had just heard; this was not the first time an outsider narrated what they had experienced. Could I possibly believe that this was not a coincidence? I recalled, a few days back, what Evan had brought to my attention. I couldn't stop tears from running down my eyes, Don looked unsure of what to say next. I told him that I noticed that he had been asking the same questions repeatedly and I assumed that it was his age catching up to him. Don shared with me that he had a father going through something similar, so he knew about Alzheimer's and its association with Dementia.

However, his father was closer to the age of 85, he was much older than Barry. Barry was in the prime of his life, he was 59, so close to his 60th birthday. I left the business stunned and dumb founded, I sat in the car and wept; it was an extremely hot day, and the little Suzuki car was so hot that I could not differentiate my tears from the sweat running down my face. I eventually turned on the car and the air conditioning as I slowly prepared to drive back. I lost it for a moment or two, and I had to pull myself together and go back to the shop. I had left my daughter there with her father as they started the afternoon clean up and preparation for the next day's trading. It was around 3 or 4 o'clock in the afternoon, I was not the same person again after that conversation; I had come to a realisation, and I just had to be more careful with my words and watch what was being said. I also started to notice the methodical ways Barry was going about his daily activities. I was watching him closely, yet I did not know what I was looking for specifically. I was mostly watching to see if I could notice any further changes. Maybe it was a turning point of awareness being told your partner was ill with a disease you could not see and only witness sporadically. It was a huge acceptance process, needless to say; I wasn't ready to accept it yet. Barry was too young to be diagnosed, I kept on telling myself; only old people get Alzheimer's!

This was when I decided to sell the shop and move out of the food industry, I had given it my best shot and tried to make it work for us, as a family. Every other thing was outside my control, I couldn't do anything to help Barry. Getting him to see a doctor was out of the question; he had never really been a man that goes to doctors. It was like a taboo to discuss such with him, especially when he makes a mistake or is not doing something right. Imagine mentioning that his mind needed to be looked at? He wasn't a bitter, nasty, or abusive person, he just felt that it was unnecessary to see a doctor if you aren't sick.

I know I had to make a firm decision on this matter, I could not keep doing this, it was not helping either of us. We put the shop on the market; by now we were close to 10 months into the twelve-month lease. We managed to keep the shop afloat for a couple of months, our daughter would come in before and after school to assist with the set up and clean-up. We kept trudging on, we could not give up because we were bound to this lease. Eventually, in late 1996 we sold our shop for well under the purchase price. I was clear of all debt and left with only $900 we lived on that till I found more work. It was a good couple of weeks while I found my footing, I had time to get some sewing done and some other things I did not have time to do since the shop opened. I was now able to pack my daughter lunch and pick her up from school. Barry had lost his job for a while now and he seemed as if he did not fully comprehend what had transpired. During the coming days, he mostly sat on a lounge chair in the living room watching TV.

It was his way of moving on from pain of having to let the shop go, he also witnessed many of my emotional nights as well. As I said before, Barry and I had a close relationship, we always talked about every little thing that arose within the family and in the household. It was not unusual for me to let off steam and tell him what was bothering me when I was really stressed out. The hardest part of it all was keeping my thoughts on Barry's health to myself because I did not want to make any hurtful assumptions.

After leaving the shop, it felt so refreshing to not have to wake up so early because I had to be at a specific place at a specific time. It took me two weeks to break out of this pattern, I was finally feeling normal again. We chose not to drive past the shop for months because we wanted to distance ourselves from that part of our life and move on.

Once again, Barry had started to show signs of absent-mindedness, he started asking the same questions over and over, even though we had answered them just minutes ago. Initially, this behaviour was sporadic, and we did not think much of it, yet as the months rolled by, it became a recurring situation. It used to be a little annoying to have the same thing asked of you several times and sometimes I would raise my voice in frustration and my daughter would bring it to my attention. This was always so painful because I was so frustrated and the whole situation was draining. Eventually I decided that it was easier to say nothing, however this also took its toll on me.

Awareness Wisdom Awakeners

◊ Sometimes sitting in quiet is good for the soul, however being able to differentiate quiet times and lost moments is difficult for the observer.

◊ Having work is a solution if partner has always been an avid worker in good substance when short period of work occur it may be an indicator that something else needs to be looked at.

◊ Find the patience within yourself to be able to persevere with the persistence in the questions as this will test you.

◊ How you respond is the best outcome for you and person asking the question. Hard as it is taking a deep breath and breath your way through, its hard I know, trust it will be ok.

◊ Be patient and do the best you can, answer in as many ways you can. Bring laughter in where you can, not to laugh at the person just to help you get through.

Chapter Six

NO Medication – Show me Another Way

There were nights when I felt my own rage burn deep inside me, I wanted to scream; the repetitive questions and the constant unresponsive answers used to drive me to an edge. I had no idea, why this was happening, nor did I really want it to it was all out of my control. I think most of my emotions had to do with the fact that I did not fully understand what was happening, and I was not ready to accept that it was real. It is heartbreaking to watch your partner of around 30+ years start to become unresponsive to the world around him. Watching this happen slowly was so heart wrenching, I could also sense my daughter's pain during those days, as she watched her dad.

What was more frustrating was that some days were good and other days were more draining, leaving us feeling disconnected from him as a family. I stayed out later than I usually do on different days because I felt so distant from Barry that it was so hard to cope every night. When the next day came, it was all forgotten and forgiven.

We had days of understanding and peace; Barry was looking at the local paper one Saturday and said that he wanted to apply for the job as the hospital mechanic. This was his trademark and as fate would have it, we did have a friend who knew of Barry and suggested that he should apply for the job.

Our focus now was to get him employed, since Barry had something to focus on, a good sign on his own momentum, however, short lived. Acceptance of his condition was about to begin being very real.

I was able to start job hunting. At this time, it had been six weeks since the shop had been sold. I walked straight back into work at the Northern Territory Government on a 6week contract in the Education Department in Winnellie Area. It proved to be perfect because our daughter would catch the bus to Winnellie from the Darwin High School and then we would drive home together. We had not sold the 2nd car as part of the sale of the shop, so it became a very useful car for running errands and job hunting. Our other car, the Mazda Bravo was being used by Barry to get to and from his own work. As luck would have it, the application for the hospital was a success, and it was only after the first 3 months' contract that we received a letter in the mail saying they were not extending Barry's contract anymore and that his employment had ceased.

When Barry lost his job, he took it hard. His working life was coming to an end, due to an illness and it was out of his control. I had to work so that we could pay the bills, and this meant that Barry had to spend most of his time on his own; at the house, watching TV. A friend who had shared the job with Barry called me one day and said that he wanted to talk to me, that there was a serious problem with Barry, and he wanted to share what he had witnessed.

"Okay Owen that is fine," I said.

"I will meet you at your place on Saturday morning to discuss what you had witnessed". We were close friends with Owen because of our shared love for tropical Orchids, it was evident that Owen and Barry had a conversation about Orchids at the local meetings we had attended. So, I knew that this meeting with Owen would be sincere and out of genuine concern. My meeting with Owen went better than I had expected, however it was not good news. As one could imagine, a hospital is full of lots of corridors and some nooks and tight spots for the engineers, mechanics, and cleaners to work and not be an interruption to the hospital usual activities. Owen started to share with me that Barry had been a good worker when his mind was on the job, and it took several people who he worked with to finally realise that his cognitive functions were not working properly. He was mostly lost in thought on numerous occasions and this was why his contract was not extended. I sat in the chair a bit stunned, was I hearing things again like previous conversations? Was I witnessing the same situation again only this time it was more direct and explained in a totally different way? I listened attentively to Owen while he was sharing his understanding of what had transpired with Barry's work. Not sure that I wanted to believe it to be true, it took a long time for it to really sink in. What was I dealing with?

I had a serious situation on my hands; how would I cope and deal with this? I had no idea what to do, or where to start. Let alone understand what this all meant for Barry. It was now evident Barry was no longer able to work on his own accord.

I thanked Owen so much, for his willingness to share with me what was happening with Barry, it didn't make it any easier, I guess the more I heard what others were witnessing, the more I started to comprehend fully what was happening. I would feel a bit lost for a while and then I would just do what I had to do and really start to take notice of the events that were occurring in front of me.

It hurt to watch and to listen to what was happening, yet I could not do anything to help because most cases if I ever questioned what was happening, I was told that there was nothing wrong with him, that it was all me.

I was wrong all along; I was the one with the problem not Barry. This usually led to anger and frustration; I let it all go, knowing that it was part of the accepting process. I had to continue what I was doing and continue living my life to the best of my ability.

Hearing repeatedly that there was nothing wrong with him, that I had the problem took its toll on me. There was always a part of me that broke every time someone said this. I knew that this was the moment I started to find myself in a moment of I want to say self-pity yet inside of me I had to be strong for myself and daughter and this was an incredibly sad emotion to witness.

I would cry myself to sleep on numerous occasions knowing that our lives were ending, and he would not recall any of the good times. I could only do the best I could, however our situation was changing and for me to cope I had to learn to step back and fall out of love with someone who had been a huge influence in my life, I had to let him go yet stay with him and guide him on so many levels. This was one of the hardest things to have to learn to do at a young age; at that time, I was around 40 years of age.

During many of the days in between I often found myself crying, this was some thing the office come to adjust to. I was hurting on so many levels and this was how I could cope; I had no idea what to do next. I lost a lot of contacts and connections in the office due to the stress of my situation. It was hard to walk in and have people know you had been crying before you get to work.

One day I was in the tea room, I had arrived in good spirits into the office however a phone call or something I witnessed just sent me over the edge, (possibly a call from Barry at home asking for something I really can't recall exactly) and I was in the kitchen area making a fresh cup when one of the other staff members come in and knew I was not in a great place. I answered good morning and they could tell by the sound of my voice I was not in a good mood. This lady became a real confide and someone I could share my thoughts with, someone I could turn to just to get through the day. Her name was Sarah, I had no idea where on the office floor she worked, all I knew was that she was a teacher who had a bad experience at a school, and she was in the head office until her situation was resolved.

What a blessing this lady would be and what great friends we have become to this day. Sarah knew I was feeling down and from memory I think she got me out of the office for some fresh air and sunshine. I shared my story (journey) with Sarah and her area of specialty turned out to be an asset to me. Sarah had studied psychology and she had a great understanding on how to assist me. Whilst this was not a subject, she taught she shared so many insights during our working days and this possibly was a huge turning point in my life. My friendship with Sarah grew and this had a significant impact on my life. Sarah and I shared so many great conversations and I found that I had a way to come back to the real world when I was around Sarah, and this was a ray of hope that encouraged me to move forward. Trust me there were some very dark days of hopelessness and with lack of understanding of what I was dealing with, I just wanted to walk away from it all. While spending time with Sarah, I was able to take a break from it all, even though I did not realize it back then.

Sometimes in life the right person shows up to lead us when we can't see our way forward anymore, and this is exactly what Sarah did, even though I wasn't aware of what was happening, it felt like the right thing to do.

I was so thankful that I crossed pathways with Sarah, and I shared this with her on several occasions. We could not be together all day; we each needed our alone time, during those times, the pain always came back. Sometimes I would be out in the garden alone or in the shower; a place I often just let the tears flow. There were times I could not distinguish tears from the shower droplets. There were some days I would come to my senses and feel human again and I would be sitting on the shower floor unaware of when I collapsed in this heap or even dropped to the floor. Sometimes I would find myself at the doctors trying to work out what the next course of action would be; trying to figure out how I would get my partner to come for an appointment. He was determined not you go to doctors. There was nothing wrong with him it was all wrong with me I needed the doctors not he was his reasoning. I still recall one conversation where our daughter tried to encourage him, and Barry's response to my daughter was that it was her mother that needed the doctor and not him. The words he said were too harsh for the ears of a young teenager. Our daughter just brushed it off and did what she had to do. She did not pressure him too much because we were unsure of what his reaction would be. We both decided that it was better to let it lie at that point in time.

By the end of 1996 Barry had pulled into himself, seemingly lost in his own world, not a lot of communication was taking place. He became a 'couch potato' in many ways, and it was not easy to be around what now appeared to be someone who was distant in so many ways.

A good friend, Mary who we knew from our previous time in the Territory had offered for Barry to mow the lawn at her place and with our lawn mower he could go there and have something to do every couple of weeks, however that caused a bit of a problem as well. It became so evident that we seemed to be using so much petrol in the Mazda Ute; I was using the smaller car for work. What was happening was that Barry still held the keys for the Ute and it was using up to 350km of fuel a day. The only reason I had knowledge about this was because I was setting the trip meter on the car every day and every night it would read between 200 and 350 km on the dial. I would ask Barry where he went to everyday, and he always told me that he never left the property; that he had not gone outside at all. One day he told me that I was imagining things, that it simply was not possible for him to be travelling that number of kilometers.

"Where would I go?" He would say.

To share a reasonable view on how long this trip would take, it was like a one-way trip to Katherine from Darwin, approximately a 4 hour's drive. Now remember Barry was a tour coach driver so driving played a huge role in his working life. Driving came easy to him; it was like a past time for him. I had no idea where he could have gone to, however I knew that getting the keys from him would be hard.

On a separate occasion, I had come home from work and found the kitchen had a funny smell to it, it was hard to recognise, then I looked on the stove, the pot placed on it was so burnt and the egg inside the pot was burnt dry. The saucepan destroyed from the heat of the stove hot plate; it had been on heat for far too long. He thought of having lunch forgot it was on the stove, I knew it had happened a couple of times because I found saucepans, pots in the rubbish bin.

As clever as it may seem, cognitive functioning during this time was sporadic and short lived. For Barry to throw the pot into the bin took some clever moments of thought, only to be totally forgotten once it had happened. I recall finding a pot into the bin and questioning why it was in the bin. Barry could not answer me, and it took a couple of good soaks and clean ups to bring it back to reasonable shape. It eventually ended up in the bin and I never retrieved it the second time. I just remembered that I had to buy a new set of pots and hide them so that I could have something to cook with when I came back from work later in the day. I think it was in the linen cupboard I kept them so that I could use them when they were needed. Sometimes I forgot to put them away and I come home from work to find that another pot had been discarded.

During the year there had been so many variations that it got to a point where I had started to take some action. I felt so alone trying to cope with things, I was a mess at work and found myself alone so many times. Even though Sarah was a huge asset she also had a job to do. Nobody had witnessed this illness among their family members and especially not in a partner nor a loved one at such a young age. I was totally on my own, apart from my daughters' support and encouragement. My boss had been very understanding, He even arranged for me to have some sessions with the work psychologist. I walked around with my head hanging low, I could not walk with a spring in my step I dragged each foot. I felt so heavy with uncertainty; how would I get out of this situation? I constantly asked myself. I tried to laugh at the office workers antics, and I wanted to cry at the same time. Crying won over every time, I was losing my partner of more than thirty plus years, and it was coming to a point he was not understanding what was happening, for us to have a relationship anymore. It was even more hurtful to see it happen in front of you, his cognitive connection of substance was waning, and I was not sure how much longer I could survive this.

When I visited my doctor, whom I had an extended conversation, and I was almost put on medication to prevent a nervous breakdown. I was strong enough to say that I did not want any medication, it would have been hard for my daughter to cope with two parents on medication, so I chose not to. I asked the doctor for other suggestions, because taking medication was out of the question. I had no idea why I thought that way at that time, medication would have been an effortless way out and a way to walk away from all my problems. I became incredibly determined on that day to focus and stay strong, because medication was out of the options. My doctor was a little bit startled, however she had a moment to think and then we sat for some time and worked on a strategy for me to complete before my next visit.

By the end of a very long teary therapist's session, I walked out of the doctor's office in a state of mind that was possibly still confused. However, I carried a piece of paper and on this paper was a list of Pros and Cons for each of our lives. I was to list the pros and cons of all aspects of our lives and bring this back to the doctor. I sat on this for a couple of days mulling it over and over in my head. Where would I start, what would I write, I was still so stressed from what I was witnessing at home let alone to write out the pros and cons of each of our lives. Daughter's Jan's and Barry's lives. I struggled with this for days. Little did I know that this whole exercise would be a huge turning point in my life for me to start seeing where I had to go next.

At first it was just thick fog; I was on a path with no direction, and I was floundering, winging it with no idea which way was right, and which was wrong. I felt so overwhelmed with this extra pressure I had no idea where to start.

Living in Darwin did have some advantages, even though it was disadvantageous that my daughter and I were coping with this alone. The rest of my family lived in Melbourne, so being able to gain a day here or there for respite was difficult. What did happen is that my daughter was now at an age where we would go out to the night clubs, and it was here that some of my frustrations were released on the dance floor. We let our hair down, sometimes we would be in the middle of the dance floor and everyone else was watching. Uncanny what used to happen on the dance floor. Certain songs being played were rhythmical enough for us to let go and just dance the night away. It may have been a couple of days after the doctor's appointment I bumped into a girlfriend whom I had not seen for several years, and she took one look at me and asked me a question.

"What is wrong Jan? You look so stressed." I took one look at my girlfriend and basically burst into tears, I practically collapsed into her arms. I felt like I was carrying the entire world on my shoulders. I had known Julie for a few years, she had worked with the same company as a secretary to the Executive Manger in an industry Barry worked in for many years ago.

I looked at Julie and shared. "You know how you saw Barry the other night at the wharf, and you didn't really get a chance to talk? Well, he is not well, and I can't cope any longer with his condition and I don't know what to do next."

I trusted Julie so much, she was like a sister to me in many ways; we had shared so many stories and we had met through Barry's work at a social event, we hit it off instantly and I was so pleased to see her on that day. We had a coffee and chatted the hour went so fast, and we both headed back to our offices and were to meet the next day.

Over the coming days during lunch meetings Julie and I looked at the pros and cons of my life, my daughter's life, and Barry's life so I could know what to do next. I had to do this, because my doctor wanted me to be admitted into the hospital to prevent a nervous breakdown. I had no one to help me and I just was going around in circles, and I could not ask our daughter to help, she was still too young. Julie's face betrayed her emotions, she had never seen this side of me before. The hour lunch break barely touched the surface however it did allow me to chat, and I was grateful for that. After talking with Julie, I shared several tears, and thanked her for her help and support. From these meetings and coffee's something transpired that allowed a way to progress and again for this I was profoundly grateful.

What transpired was Julie offered to scribe for me in a way that I could just talk my way through things, and she would note it all down. It was such a relief to have such a friend offer to do this, it had me feel a huge relief internally, though I had no idea what would transpire into words when we did the exercise. Julie met with me for several days to have lunch and we had shared some catch up stories and I bought her up to speed in what I had witnessed with Barry's decline.

It took her several days to really get her head around it as well because she had worked in an office close to Barry's work and she knew of the manager's views and what they thought of Barry. So, to hear the news that he was now losing his mind was hard to accept and comprehend to a fellow ex worker. During the following couple of weekends, Julie and I met at her place, and we just let the day flow with no real expectations on what the outcomes would be. I just wanted to feel free, to feel a sense of control over my life, so that I could gain insight into our family life. This was extremely hard to do for three people, when you felt so lost about your own life. However, it was her offer to scribe for me that really helped and made me feel like I was making progress.

It took us a while to get into full swing, we listened to music and talked in general and then from memory, Julie asked a question so innocently and it made our conversation take some shape and we proceeded to complete all the suggested questions that the doctor had asked of me.

How does one answer questions for someone else's life? How did I know what they wanted? One of the hardest things was to sit objectively as if I was in their shoes at that point in time and ask myself the same questions repeatedly. I felt my heart sinking once again; how was I to know all of this? How was I to know what was best for them? I was not sure how I managed all this. All I know was that having Julie there to help write down my answers made me feel like a burden was lifted from my shoulders. I just let the words flow on that day as much as I could I wanted this exercise to work and it did for me, even though it was draining, it was worth it.

I do not remember the direct questions however some of them went in this order:

1. What were the good things working well in my life at that moment: the things with which worked for my life, Barry's life and for Daughter's life?

2. List three things I am happy with in life for Barry and Daughter, then expand to five things, or as many as I could?

3. Who did I know to be of assistance to move forward, for Barry and Daughter and my life?

4. Where in life was I now, also for Barry and for Daughter?

5. What were the things I was unhappy with in life at this moment for the three of us?

6. What did I feel in this moment a feeling of heaviness, loss of breath? What was causing the heavy feeling.

Others may have easily answered these questions, yet I had to dig deep, and make use of my inner strength to find the answers. Due to Julie's past association with Barry, she was always encouraging me to dig deeper to find the truth, and this was the sum of the whole exercise. A difficult and hard exercise to do and one that caused a lot of tears and pain, yet somehow, I got through it. I wanted to find the answers, even if they did not appear instantly, it was all going in the right direction.

The same questions were to be answered for my daughter, I was to list the highs and lows of a mother witnessing my daughter going through such pain and then list what I could do to help.

Then it was the time to answer the same questions in the column for Barry. What were the highs and lows of his life?

The overall question I had to face was, what can I do about this? And how can I make this an easy path to walk? If I did one thing every day towards getting the best outcome for us all? Take one step every day, do something towards getting better care for him and make sure he is safe while I'm at work. Barry's overall condition was to be considered first, next was my health and my daughters health. We had to know what was wrong with Barry, I had to be strong and lend the rest of my immediate family some of my strength so that we can all move forward. It was not an easy task to do on my own and yet I had to do it alone. Julie had a husband to attend to and my daughter and I had each other so we used this as our backbone to stay on the path.

I know it took several hours for this all to come through and Julie was able to note a lot down that helped see the overall picture. With tears streaming down my face and a sigh of relief we decided we had conquered a huge mountain on that day, we put our pencils down and headed to the pool with a drink. We proceeded to strip down and go for a swim in the pool, Julie opened a bottle of wine, and I truly don't recall how or when I got home; I think it was the next day.

Now that this was completed, I felt relief because I could walk into my doctor's office with a bit if a smile on my face. The next course of action was to get Barry to the doctor's office for assessment, so that we could see what the next step was.

I can't recall what the overall outcome was with the Doctor on the next visit, I just remembered that I was on the right path after doing the exercise. If I recall correctly, the doctor was so surprised at my responses, she was only too happy to refer me to Alzheimer's Association to move forward and I knew that I was strong enough to take the next step.

Awareness Wisdom Awakeners

◇ Having good friends to be there when you need them the most is the most pleasing experience to witness, and I am forever grateful to Julie for her assistance it helped me ten-fold.

◇ The doctor may always suggest a pill as a solution always know there are other ways to handle the situation yes it may get tough however you will achieve more than you ever set out to do.

◇ Never force any situation, the aim is to achieve the outcome. Forcing will not cover all the aspects you need to and so hence maybe end up doing it twice.

◇ Learn to trust your own inner strength.

◇ Your judgement is an indicator of the steps for you to take, they will be right for you trust your own judgement. Trust your internal voice and your intuition.

Chapter Seven

Doctor's Assessment

No matter what I tried; Barry was not getting any better. And getting him to a doctor was harder than I had anticipated. I had to lie that getting a complete assessment from the doctor was a requirement if he wanted his pension. I remember using this same strategy to get him to see the family doctor.

Even though we had tried several times, he dug his heels in and refused to go, this meant that we had to cancel the appointment so that the doctor was aware that we were not going to make it. He did not see anything wrong in going to the specialist for his tablets to curb his Parkinson's, but to go to the normal GP was a different story. I can't recall exactly what was happening, and I think we were out one day, and I rang the doctors to see if there was an appointment free for us to visit. I was close to the doctor's office, so it proved to be a perfect time. Barry had reluctantly accepted to come along at that time, fortunately for us, the waiting room empty. This was great because Barry seemed to shy away from crowded places. I called my daughter and told her that I had finally gotten her dad to the doctors, all we had to do now was wait.

What happened at the doctors totally shocked me in many ways because my partner's response to general questions from the doctor really did not warrant the level of frustration and aggression that was shown.

I recall the doctor looking at me a couple of times as he could not work out the anger either so we both just kept moving forward. Barry seemed so frustrated by all the questions the GP was asking. I had visited the GP several times prior, so he was totally aware of the depth of what we were looking at and how to get it all to come together.

Our GP was a caring man and he made progress to record Barry's condition. The doctor was so helpful and did a full assessment of all cognitive and normal functionality to access his comprehension. I sat in on the appraisal, the GP would ask questions of common sensibility and simple arithmetic questions and general knowledge. He tested for items of recall and memory test. It was not good; one item if any was noted even out of only 5 items so that lead to short term memory problems being diagnosed.

The answers Barry responded to all other questions were very blunt and with some element of anger, the doctor asked the necessary questions, and my partners response was mostly.

"Don't know; Don't care; Don't want to know" His responses really had the doctor and I worried. I had no idea he was not aware of his everyday surroundings; he was just sitting in front of the television 24/7. It became so obvious that he was not absorbing anything. This was a huge wakeup call for me and a day of much pain, I also realized what was really happening right in front of me. I was told by the doctor that life would begin to change from now on as my partners condition was now evident, he would need a psychiatrist assessment, and this would lead him to the next phase where he would be placed in a home to be cared for.

Witnessing things in front of me really had my heart sink, because now I could see from the assessment that I did have a huge problem on my hands. I had to figure out how to deal with things and to keep the flow of everyday life steady so that I did not lose my own functionality. Reality started to sink in further, I was now ready to hear and accept the level of illness my partner was at. Hard as it was to hear, I had already conditioned myself to fall out of love with Barry to make it easier for me to cope, I could detach myself from the emotion I was feeling on some level. Tears would still well up inside me as he progressed and witnessing everything just made it hard for all of us to adjust to. I recall one day when my daughter and I had a bit of a spat because I was so frustrated, she yelled at me saying that I was being a bit hard on Barry, I felt really hurt that she would say that. When Barry was allowed to leave the doctors room, he walked straight outside and just stared into space, it was evident that something was not right; all he could say to me was that now that he had come out of the doctor's office, he wanted to go home.

I was already red-eyed and feeling so much pain and hurt and frustration from this whole experience, perhaps it was about now that I started asking myself 'why me?' 'Why is this happening to me?' 'What can I do?' If anything, I just truly wanted to run, yet my head and my heart would not move in that direction. I was here to assist to the best of my ability, it would have been the coward's way to run, even though it felt like the easiest way out.

I drove home slowly yet really re appraising all the answers to what the GP had asked Barry and it was so hard to hear those words - "don't know don't care don't want to know". I had met and fallen in love with a man who was like my encyclopaedia he was a very sharp man with a lot of knowledge about the happenings in the world.

Here I was driving a man that did not want to know or care about anything anymore. I had no real idea about what was going on with him and he was not in a place to share these thoughts with me himself. If ever I did ask a question, I was told that there was nothing wrong with him, that it was me that something was wrong with. The silence in the car was deafening on some level yet I was trying to work out my own feelings whilst I drove.

I felt internally gutted, yet Barry just sat motionless in the passenger seat, it was like he could not find the words to express his anger. How do you know what to say or even how to think straight when a loved one has been diagnosed with a huge mental illness? What words can describe it? Not many words were said in the drive home which lasted around 45 mins in peak hour. These were very lonely times.

This was also very hard for my daughter of 15 years, she had to watch her dad as he slowly deteriorated. It was a very trying time for us both because she was at that age where children started to get independent; in many ways, we depended on each other, she was my rock. My daughter was also going through a lot at school, she was missing most of her classes; the school called me one day saying that they were genuinely concerned at the levels of stress they witnessed in such a young girl. The career councillor talked to me on the phone, and it was only days after the assessment was known and confirmed by the doctor, I was struggling with myself, so I had no idea what was happening with our daughter. I was not aware that she could feel my pain and that of her dad. A fifteen-year-old should not have to witness such, yet there she was, right in the middle of all this.

The Career councillor shared what she had witnessed, and this upset me as well, it was evident that she was ringing to confirm what my daughter was sharing. She also wanted to know if there was anyone that could watch over her. As a mother you may be able to imagine how that felt, I was not able to turn to any one either, so we only had each other. It was around this time that we were guided to the Alzheimer's Association for assistance and guidance. Now that Barry's condition had been confirmed, it was much harder to develop time for ourselves, to sit and chat or discuss anything we wanted to share.

Since we were in Darwin by ourselves, we had no family there who could assist us. I still have no idea how I managed, I just kept going. There were days when things were so tough that I thought I couldn't cope, all I could do was drive or go and sit on the banks of the foreshore and write letters to a friend I met in the navy, it was this time I spent by myself not going home till it was late or even dark. I did not want to go home I just felt like my life was being cut into two and one half of me was dying. In fact, I was, Barry and I had a long relationship, and it was over 28+ years by now. This was a hard way to witness losing your partner and the father of your child.

The months passed, and the days rolled on, I started to find the strength to investigate building a house. There was a completely new subdivision just south of Darwin and I had a goal to aim for, I wanted to build a house on one of the blocks. This was a huge goal to aim towards especially when you are under extreme stress. I was extremely determined, I wanted to live in my own house again, so I set out to make it happen. Since I worked at a government office, my income was consistent, so I applied for government assisted home loans.

I managed to secure a loan and then found a property and a builder to build my home, during all this Barry just followed me around like a puppy, he was still driving several kilometres a day and yes things were still being burnt on the stove. I know this from the pots I found in the bin one day and he had no explanation as to how it got there.

From the experience with the GP, I was eventually contacted by a psychiatrist who would also do an assessment, and this would then be another step into Barry's condition and possible placement in a home. I had no other option because I still needed to work to put food on the table and pay all the bills. At one point it was suggested by family members that I should stay home and manage from home, however my comments were would you live on $365 a fortnight carers payment. I needed a life as well and I was doing the best I could for both my daughter and my partner. I needed to work to stay on top as well. After the psychiatrist assessment I was presented with a full comprehensive report, and this was then more confirmation about Barry's condition. I was told by the doctor and psychiatrist that life would begin to change from now on as partners, since his condition was now more evident, he would need some additional care. This was also the next step that would lead him to the next phase of placement into a home of care. At least I could ask for some help and a carer to take Barry out of the house once a week, while I was at work.

We managed each day as it was presented to us. I was now working 3 jobs concurrently: one being a full-time government worker in administration. I was working nights in Woollies, part time; I spent the night packing shelves and I also had a casual job where I had a manifest of letters to post on certain days. This all kept me extremely busy, I needed to keep my head above water and keep my own mind active. I was also running on adrenaline as I did not sleep very much;

I spent a lot of time in chat rooms on the internet just looking for companionship. I wanted to share my story with others as a means of coping.

I received a very distressed call from my daughter one day, only a short time after the assessments were completed. This rang bells to me that we had now a sense of loss that was possibly more than any one had imagined. One point during this whole experience my daughter witnessed something very real for her, it was to be an indication of Barry's loss of time in his life to the life he was now in.

My daughter had arranged for a meeting with a girlfriend at the movies, her friend was to call with a time and location. When her friend called that afternoon, Barry got to the phone first and answered it.

"Hello," my said daughter's friend, eager to talk to her. "Hello, who are you looking for?"

There was a pause, then after a while, he said.

"Sorry, there is nobody here, you must have the wrong number" then he hung up the phone. Our daughter was standing less than six feet away from her father and asked.

"Who was that?"

"Oh" he said, as if he didn't see her there "it was someone looking for Lori" confused by her presence.

"But I am that person."

He replied. "I have no idea who you are and what you are doing in my house?"

She must have been so shocked to witness what had just happened; Barry moved to sit back down as if nothing happened. I then get a call from my daughter, sounding distressed, she proceeded to share what she had witnessed. Daughter was 15 years of age and Barry had no recollection of her in his life, it had only been a short 2 years since everything all started from our first authentic experience. There was not a lot we could do; we now had an indication that he had lost 15 years of his own life. We had no idea where to go to next, we just lived with it each day until things become clearer.

Daughter was feeling this pain just as much as I was however with my own life being strained, I omitted to see that my daughter was not coping as well, and she was looking for love and reassurance that I could not give due to my own level of stress. I had witnessed that school was suffering, and she was also ready to spread her own wings, I could not stop her, and I was not in a place to be too stern as it was hard enough for her to witness what was happening let alone put constraints on her during this time.

My daughter had become resistant to any request that had been asked of her because she was starting to mature in her own way. She found herself involved with a different group of people and while they were nice and friendly, it was not the lifestyle we had chosen for her as she was growing up. However, it was a lesson in life she had to learn at that time. A series of events led us down the path of her being hospitalised for a short period of time it was here we found out she was pregnant under the age of 16.

This just about drove me to a point of no return. What had I done to deserve this?

Coping with my daughter's situation and my partner losing his mind from dementia was not the best way to spend your daughter's 16th birthday, however it was what it was.

Awareness Wisdom Awakeners

◇ Be very mindful of others around you, everyone has their own way of coping; no one is right nor they wrong, its merely different perspectives.

◇ Really listen and watch for the attention that children are seeking – it's hard to pick up on everything. It is sharing love that helps the child to cope and to have someone help you as well even outside of the home for your own strength and preservation.

◇ Avoid being afraid to seek help, it does not mean you are weak it truly means you are at the end of your tether and seek help, so things make a change. Better to ask than have yourself fall in a crumbled heap. There is no sense in this situation.

◇ Its ok to take time for you. You owe yourself this it helps you to stay strong for you. That's the most important thing you can do.

Chapter Eight

Worried More than I Realised

One of my biggest concerns in life was the impact all of this had on my daughter. I didn't see it then however I can now; I lost my way on so many occasions from my own stress level and while I was trying to keep myself afloat, I lost sight of what was really happening to my daughter. It was not intentional it was just what happened. We had witnessed something during our lifetime that an average person would not be ready to witness, especially at the age of sixteen. Most times we needed our own space, even if we had each other to confide in.

Coping with the pregnancy came with a new level of stress that caused a rift between my daughter and I. Being separated from my daughter pushed me to my limits. I did everything a mother would do to protect her daughter however in this case a situation occurred where it bought a lot of pain to us both and my daughter needed love in so many other ways. While I write this from my perspective at the time it was a hard subject to approach. We both had a huge amount of stress in each of our lives and we lost sight of each other for a while.

We did have an enormous argument and I will not go any further than to say, my daughter saw the light and was able to make an informed decision that had her terminate the pregnancy.

Which also allowed for her life to come back to a sense of normality regarding the situation we were dealing with. As a mother it was not an easy thing to witness my daughter coping with this as well as the loss of her dad.

The months moved on and it became evident that I needed to make a move to trade the ole' Mazda in as a way of stopping Barry from driving. We did have one incident when I arrived home to an empty house. This caused a lot of worry because we had no idea where to start to look for Barry. This was possibly the turning point to ascertain control and to bring his touring to an end. It became a necessity for me to start to look for a car that would serve a purpose. It was also evident that his conditions were not conducive with the laws, and we needed to get the keys for the car from him. Barry had become very protective of the keys, and I had to develop a way so that I could gain access to the car and trade it.

Behind the scenes I was already looking at several yards and doing test drives with several cars and it was not an easy job to do when you are a woman in a car yard. During previous times I was always grateful to Barry because I had learnt a lot from him even though the pushy car salesman coming and thinking he could influence the woman for an easy buy. The salesman for each yard learnt that I was different.

The one thing that was extra clever that I thought of was opening the hood of the car and listening to the engine. I would always ask the salesman to start the car and I would have my head under the hood, listening to the engine. I always got questioned whether I knew what I was doing. I would answer that it was for me to know and for them to figure out. I did not want them to think that I was one of those women that did not know about cars.

Now I did this so convincingly that they did not know if I knew about cars or was just bluffing. Just where I wanted them to be. I would ask all the technical questions I could think of because this is what I learnt from Barry. What the salesman did not know about me is that I was Barry's left-hand man when he worked on many engines, and I learnt a lot about the mechanics and operations of engines as he pulled engines down and rebuilt them.

Let alone assist in the engine installation of a Diesel Turbine Generator of a Ferry he and I worked on. Grease and all I had used some tools at some point in time on engines with Barry.

So, I bluffed my way through, then the day come to decide which car was I going to take.... I have played the salesman perfectly into my hand. I had 3 cars I was juggling with all of which eligible to do a swap for the same car value I was trading in with the Mazda. I can't recall the models however the car I eventually took was the car I gave the least amount of follow up in pretesting. I used it as the prime car and ran test on the others against it one by one. The salesman thought it was going for the gold car when in fact I said as I stood in front of the Toyota Corolla that I was taking this one and tuned to the Corolla as I shared my decision. My daughter's boyfriend was the only other male that drove the car as he had the technical knowhow about the running of the car to give me a male's perspective and we tested all three cars this way. So, the salesman thought I was going for a lessor car then the car I chose. To this day he still shares with me I had him bluffed he had no idea of my experience and he complimented me on my ability to choose a car non influenced by the salesman.

I had shared with the salesman what my intention was and how I foresaw the sale taking place. Whilst he had empathy for me it was agreed I would get the Mazda appraised and this would be the price of the car I would purchase.

So, around the $15,000 trade value was agreed. It was an easy swap over, and I was so grateful the sales yard was co-operative to my situation. Trust me some of them were not!

I had taken a day when out driving with Barry for groceries that I wanted to go to a car yard, and I had the phone number of the sales guy ready to let him know when I would visit so it was all lined up in advance. I had no idea what day it would be only that I would get the car to him for appraisal during the week and he and I would do the business and then I would get the car there for transfer. It all seemed to go to plan. Then getting the keys was a different story from Barry.

It became crunch time at home to get the keys access for the Mazda to use for the trade in. I was not expecting to end up in hospital from this experience nor loose a couple of days recuperating.

As I have mentioned Barry was protective of the car keys. I had set up a plan and process that indicated we needed to downsize the car as it was now too large a car and we did not need it for camping, nor any other purpose and it was now a time for the car to be changed. Of course, this caused some momentarily comments which were forgotten very soon after the conversation however it was not easy to have nor keep flowing when there was so much confusion as well in the mix. I was able to draw on the fact that Barry was with me the day of appraisal and he knew it was happening however he always referred I was not there and knew nothing about a change over.

A hard call however one I had to play on to get the keys. What had transpired in the house for Daughter, and I was that she was now with her licence, and she would use the little Suzuki Hatch we had from the shop, and I would use the Mazda as the main car then trade it in for the Toyota I had agreed on. The morning arrived and I was bopping along and making some form of conversation when I asked Barry for the keys of the Mazda to which he made a move to get them.

The day had come to give the car a good clean and ready to go to the yard for the trade-in-swap over; I was going to do in the coming week. It did not all go to plan I ended up at the hospital. I know, I lost about two whole days recouping.

I remember being able to get the keys; my daughter and boyfriend were still in bed after a late night out, however I recall calling desperately for their help and assistance as Barry was not willing to give me the keys from his hands.

I think I took a swoop to get them, and this ended up with us in a form of wrestling each other for the keys, I know we ended up in the hallway and a foot mark was imprinted on the door as Barry took defence to not let me get to his pocket. I know I ended up outside screaming for help as with the bang on the bedroom door caused for my daughter's boyfriend (now husband), who also approached Barry as best we could he ended up with a few small swings and tempers flaring under the heated situation that was occurring.

Neighbours had to have heard the commotion and voices screaming as next I knew the police were standing at the door. I know I was very distressed from all the situation and to see the police really had me crumble inside.

Barry did own a shot gun and I was asked by the police as a standard question were there any firearms in the house? I was also asked what was the situation occurring in the household? I began to explain what was happening. One of the police searched for the gun in Barry's room and found the firearm behind the bed so that was removed quickly.

Barry had no recollection it was gone so never asked after it again.

I also explained what our situation was and noted that everything had quieted down with Barry since the police were on the scene, he seemed to be his normal self again. The police were happy with the situation and left the premise asking for me to go and fill in the forms at the station in a day or so for the gun to be surrendered. Barry was not able to complete the paperwork so I said I would be there within the 7 days to complete the transaction. I was not aware of what was about to take place that would have me lose 2 days of my life practically sleeping to gain my strength and composure back.

Awareness Wisdom Awakeners

◇ There can be high feelings of tension when in a place that you need to take control of something, always have someone else with you if you can. Getting the keys was a difficult task and it was lots of teamwork that helps to make it as easy as possible for the patient.

◇ The short-term memory is incredible as they patient doesn't have the recall ability to remember and so reverts to a natural calm state. NB every patient will be uniquely different to their situation.

◇ Getting the control to do what you must do is not an easy thing to cope with let alone take control of the situation. You must be strong in self to make those decision and know you are doing everything in the best interest of the person concerned. To others it may not look like it however they are not in your shoes. Do everything you have to for the best outcome for the person who needs care.

Chapter Nine

Inconsolable

From my memory as soon as the police were gone, the boyfriend took a leap at Barry, which took him totally by surprise while no violence occurred nor assault, the boyfriend managed to get hold of the car keys from his pocket. Before I knew what was happening, the boyfriend threw the keys to me, and I was outside the house crying my heart out while driving away as fast as I could.

The jump on Barry had his hand fall from his pocket with the keys in it and the keys landed on the floor. The boyfriend threw the keys to me and told me to go.

LEAVE.

I was a little startled by this event and with tears streaming down my face I stood for a minute waiting for the outcome to subside however Barry realised he was now without the keys and started to make a move towards me. All I heard in the surrounding noise and voices was go just go you have the keys now GO. I can't recall if my daughter witnessed this all however it was her voice I heard to go when I finally moved and moved fast.

I could not say how I got to the car or where it was parked, I just know I was in the car very quickly I just wanted to be out of the situation and run. Where would I go, I recall driving for a period maybe 10 minutes, maybe 20, time was irrelevant for me.

I was so distressed and feeling so much in pain from what had to be done to get the keys, it was dangerous for me to be on the road. Yet here I was just slowly cruising the streets, roaming aimlessly.

Bakewell was a new subdivision and I ventured down some streets that I had no idea even existed some months earlier. I did have some friends in a neighbouring suburb however I was unsure how to approach them I was still sobbing and by now the shock of all that had occurred was making my body tremble and I felt so alone and unsure how could I stay in this situation I needed help.

It took a lot to stop the car to regain composure and letting the car start to roll before I eventually come to a complete stop outside my friend's house. I recall walking so wobbly towards the door if anyone knew me and saw me, they could have thought I was drunk however I was now feeling weak and totally exhausted from this whole incident, I found enough strength to bang on the friend's door. I did not know however that they were still in bed. I kept banging and calling out "Robyn, Mark". I was still crying and feeling so unsure of myself and what was happening to me. I have never been in this situation in my life, and I did not understand the emotions I was going through. What was happening to me is all I could think of and then there was the thought of what was happening back at the house. My daughter was still at the house I hoped she was okay. What could be happening to them?

I was too weak to call and when I say weak, I mean weak in my own strength. I had started to collapse to the floor when the door opened, and two startled people were looking at me wondering what on earth I was doing; had I lost my mind. As the door opened, I stood there saying words that even I could not comprehend.

I finally made it to the couch or a chair in the house. I just sat on the chair rocking back and forth jabbering to myself, muttering nothing of constructive sentences. I know I did say call Daughter, to tell her where I am... I have no idea if this took place however something must have happened as next, I recall drinking water and being asked questions. And bit by bit things started to take shape of the events as they transpired from my thoughts. I was in a place that I felt safe, yet I had no idea what was happening to me inside. I could not stop shaking and I could not stop rocking back and forth. My words slurred and one could say I was drunk however not from alcohol, but from sheer mental exhaustion and totally fatigue.

Why I went to Robyn's' and Mark's house on that day; I really have no idea, it was just something that happened. I had worked with Robyn in the office, and she had an idea of what was happening, however no real concept of the full situation. I had no idea of what Robyn and Mark would do but luckily for me, they were friends with a particularly good doctor, and they were able to call him to access my situation.

I was inconsolable. I was in this state for several hours that I can recall. I did calm down after fresh water and some food, but it was the trip to the hospital that had me really get a grip of where I was, and I just kept crying. I asked myself severally if I was losing my mind? If I was going to a place I might never return from. I really could not gather my thoughts at that point in time. I sat in the car and just stared out the window as the streets passed by.

I know I was at the hospital; on some level I slept with my eyes open all the way. I did not know what was next, it was a very scary part of my life that I would never wish onto anyone. We made it to the emergency rooms at the hospital and we sat for several minutes till my name was called, I may have seemed a bit dazed because I seem to recall Robyn assisting me to a cubicle. The doctor was a young man from what I remember, and, on numerous occasions, he would bring in another doctor to discuss how I was progressing health-wise. In the end I know my friends were given some pills and told what to do with them. They were told that I had to be in someone's care for a while. I know I shed more tears as I shared with the Doctor what was happening and where I was in life, and I really do not know if they understood or not or if it was something they had not dealt with before.

I do not recall getting out of the hospital or much else from that day I know the next comprehending moment was when I woke up to go to the restroom and it was dark. I felt a bit groggy and being in a strange place, I had to call for some assistance so that I knew where I was. My daughter was nowhere to be seen and Robyn come to the room. I recall drinking more water and having food and sleeping till the next morning. If I remember correctly, Daughter and her boyfriend came to pick me up the next day and take me home so that I could recuperate in my own home.

All I can recall about the returning home was that when I asked my daughter and her boyfriend what happened to Barry after I left with the car. The boyfriend told me that after I left with the car, Barry immediately went back to his chair to sit in front of the TV and never asked about the keys or the car. Getting the car sorted out was the beginning of a long road.

It felt good to be back home again, even though I had lost a couple of days, I was ready to get my life back on track.

Awareness Wisdom Awakeners

◇ Take time out to reflect on where you are at, sleep is a good healer.

◇ Find someone you can trust and not judge you or control your movements. You must be in control of you all the time, some elements of alertness are good for your soul.

◇ Sometimes there will be hard decisions to make. Avoid other people's comments advice unless they are qualified in the arena. Ask yourself is this decision right for my situation.

Chapter Ten

Finding Hope and Healing

After a whole weekend of events and after a couple of days from work, life gained some normality. I started to get back into shape the next hurdle to cross was to wait for the psychiatrist assessment to be done and to learn as much as I could on what next steps I could take to keep moving forward in the best interest for Barry's outcome. I had visited the Alzheimer's Association on numerous occasions as a way of coping and as a way of learning with what I was dealing.

This proved to be a testing time, as I also needed a break (a holiday); I needed to get away, to gather my strength. It took many months to put all this in order, but once I had a strategy and plan from the assessment of the psychiatrist, everything else was easy. The Alzheimer's Association had been able to accommodate Barry into a couple of their facilities to help my daughter and I, however on one of the two occasions, it become evident that Barry could not stay because there was not enough security on ground, we found out that he kept escaping.

I had to be at work every day and I needed to arrange for meals on wheels to come for at least lunch most days so that Barry had something to eat. It was not that there was nothing in the fridge it was that he sometimes did not remember to feed himself.

My daughter was a huge help when she was at home at mealtimes, but most times, work took precedence for us both.

The day come for the assessment of the psychiatrist to take place. I was aware of the event occurring, however when the man come to the door Barry defences went up because there was a strange man in his house. He sat at the table, and we had a cuppa in the early greeting to encourage Barry to participate in the conversation I had previously been advised by the psychiatrist that it would be an assessment, that I did not need to be there once he had made a connection with Barry. This took about20 mins and then I just slipped out the door and left them there chatting. It was all arranged, and I was away from the house for about an hour.

During this time the psychiatrist would assess the comprehension and processing faculties in Barry's brain. He had to answer several questions and do a memory test. He looked at his gait and his stance, it was all part of the assessment. Trust me when I read the word gait in the report, I wondered what gait was and I was amazed to learn it was how he walked that was also assessed. A truly thorough assessment had taken place. I returned to the house to find that Barry and the Psychiatrist were just coming to the end of their meeting. Whilst Barry thought of this man as a new friend, he would never be seen again. The report arrived in the mail several days later and it was in reading the report that the truth would sink in even further. What we had witnessed were all signs of the disease called Alzheimer's Dementia.

It was at this time that I think I fully became aware of the impact this disease was having on Barry. How powerful is the mind and what was happening to Barry now?

It was a thought that crossed my mind on several occasions. What eventuated from this experience was that I did go searching to gain a full understanding of this disease.

The doctor received the report and so did the Alzheimer's Association. The level of Barry's condition warranted some assistance to endeavour to get him into a home. What become very evident is that there were no secure homes in Darwin that he could stay; the ones that were available were full, so I had to look for a home in another state. This proved a little awkward on many occasions as while Barry did have family members in another state, he was estranged to them, and communication was at a minimum. The other states were hesitant in answering my questions.

This become a huge concern for me as it was evident that I was going to need a lot of more assistance and guidance on how to get him to an interstate home. I did have some holidays coming up and I could see that I would need to use that time to travel to Melbourne in particular.

As the days rolled on, I experienced an incident where a friend called me up to say that Barry was at their place; he was heading to Melbourne. He did not have any money on him there was no provision for food nor was there a case for clothing, and he was adamant of travelling to Melbourne. Alarm bells were ignited. Firstly, how on earth did he get to the friend's place around 10 mins drive south of Palmerston, and what car was he in?

When I asked how Barry got to the friend's place, he said he was in the white Suzuki car. The friends were aware of the situation. We had no idea that Barry had enough skill to find his way to his friend's home, they were able to keep him there till my daughter was able to take him home.

This was a huge cause for alarm, unexpectantly Barry seized a moment to pick up the keys for the Suzuki car that our daughter was now driving. She had left the keys for a short period of time on the bench, while she attended to something else. It was a quick move on Barry's part, the scary part as I recall was that Barry left whilst daughter was still in the house, so she had no idea where he had gone to. He was not in the house, and neither was the car. This did have a huge impact on me as well as daughter and we were in a spin for a good hour we had no idea where to start to look for him before our friend rang us with news Barry was at his place.

I had done everything I could to get his licence revoked however this never happened because Barry would not do the test at the Main Roads Department where they assess his comprehension for driver's licence. I was dealing with this, incident really proved how careful my daughter and I had to be with the keys. On receiving the phone call from our friend to say Barry was at his place heading for Melbourne; it was with a sigh of relief, now my daughter and I headed to his friend's place.

Once we arrived Barry was automatically back to his old self and got back into the Suzuki to travel back home. When we were leaving the friend's place it was evident from conversation that Barry thought he was on his way to Melbourne, and he just didn't know how much further it was to go. Our friends become a wee bit over judgemental and made some strong remarks we were overreacting to the situation, this caused for a few words to be said and the stress of this caused for our friendship to cease as of that moment. Hard and all as it was, some friend had made comments on our actions and it was hard to share what was really happening when they kept seeing the man, they thought they knew not the man he had become.

They were not with him 24/7 nor were they dealing with the situation of his habits and what we had witnessed. As with all adversities you really find out who the true friends are when in a situation of this kind and to be honest with you, it also showed us how many people had their own perception of what they thought was happening not what was happening. Family members were a little the same. To be honest with you this was my daughter's father, and he was my partner, friend, buddy. It was hard to witness the judgement when others made comments on something they were not involved with nor living with.

For me this was a huge sign of remission in his life, if in 2 years of diagnosis he had lost 15 years with no recollection of his daughter, then we were starting to deal with his return to Melbourne life where he grew up and spent a good part of his life. It was his later years that he spent in Darwin, and this now seemed to have been forgotten. Barry was no longer fully involved in our conversations, so it was hard to work with him when he no longer shared any of his feelings or his thoughts.

This incident taught us that we had to be very careful with the car keys and always keep them on us. We could not have this happen again. It was a scary time and yet it was also a time to really reflect where he was on his journey down the road of Alzheimer's.

My daughter had witnessed a lot of stress and strain to be losing her dad this way and I took it upon myself to work through the next decision in a very stressful time on my own. I have no idea other than to say I was endeavouring to protect daughter from any more stress; however, she was also my rock and to be honest we did share a lot of things on this whole journey together. We only had each other to cope so we had to be open.

The entire process was not easy to deal with. Because I know I had witnessed this last situation it become a very high focus for me to seek other opportunities to have Barry placed in a home in Melbourne. The actual memories of what I did first here are not clear, all I can share is that I had numerous conversations with several people in the mental health department and in the Alzheimer's Association. These meetings were to share with me where I could locate places for Barry to be excepted. I still had to make all the enquiries and make all the contacts, so it was a huge job of collecting information and trying to sort through it all to decide. This really had a huge impact on me in many ways, I had to really take control of his life to get him settled. I had to share a lot of information about his condition and from memory I had to fill in a lot of forms to be able to be accepted into these homes. Once I found a place, I would then share that information with the mental health area, I think this was so that they could send the official psychiatrist assessment down validating Barry's condition.

Trust me this was a very gruelling time; it was hard to focus on my own life and share with daughter and to cope with my own internal feelings. I sometimes would turn to unwind with company of a male, this was my only way to feel human again when I was in the middle of stress. I often felt lost and alone and could not really talk to many as nobody else had had to deal with a situation of this kind, so I was walking a thin line of what of? What do I do? Where do I go next?

I needed to ask myself these questions repeatedly to get through the day. I know I chatted a lot online as the internet had a variety of chat rooms and I found myself in one of these several nights, I had to air my thoughts and the chat rooms became a way to do this.

Initially I was against my daughter going on the internet, as it was so new, and one did not know what to gain from it, however, for me, it became an essential part of my day as I would use the computer at work for eight hours and then I would come home and chat online for another eight to twelve hours. It was amazing the number of chats that I came across with people that were in similar situations, however, most of the people were much older. Even though they could relate to my situation, it was someone they could walk away from, it was either their grand parent or older parent, not many of them were dealing with a partner. I remember one chat I had led me to an overseas group that dealt with Alzheimer's and Dementia, this group helped me a lot. I can't recall any specifics however I just know it led me to be able to cope with another day and take another step. I got to chat with people who understood the situation and shared tips that helped me move forward every day.

I have no idea where this group is today, and it was an asset for me at the time. Barry and my sleeping arrangements had changed significantly, and I was in a room on my own, the computer was there as well I slept on a fold up bed and trust me those nights of humidity did take its toll on me. It was not un-common for me to wake and get out of the bed and sit for several hours, chatting on the computer. Only to get one or two hours sleep and then go to work. It was normal for me since it was adrenaline I was running on. My diet had changed as well, even though I'm not a fast-food lover, these meals did assist in the time of stress as I did not come home to cook for self. I would go walking up to two hours after work sit and write on some nights, sitting at a picnic table that overlooked the Darwin harbour. It was here I could find my own space to think.

I was outdoors and despite being alone I was dumping a lot of stuff on paper, so this also helped me to stay on track and pen down some of my thoughts. Some of the days I would meet my girlfriend here and we would have a laugh and walk the trail to East Point on the foreshore.

I knew I was running on something however what it was I was not sure, for me it was just something I did an everyday I would follow suit, it just seemed the normal thing to do. I had no idea what it would do to me nor if it would have any effect on my body in the long run of things. It just felt normal for me. I was feeding on the adrenaline for a long time it was what helped me stay on track, I think. My boss at work was aware of my emotional state and this helped me a lot as there were days when I was a mess and other days when I felt on top of the world. I was not aware of the highs and lows in life I used to say as each day come forth. It was like climbing a ladder - some days would be three rungs and fall back two, other days it would be two rungs and fall back 2, one day I said its one step today just to get through today and to those that heard me say this would love my positive attitude to stay on track. The average comment was "I got to hand it to you Jan I could not do what you are doing. You are an inspiration". I never knew what that meant at the time as I felt such a heavy load, I was just doing what I could to get through each day. I kept on having a positive attitude even though many of my days were heavy and low, and people did know.

Internally, I was angry and confused as to why was this happening to me; inside I hurt because of the loss of my partner after 35 years. And some days I was selfish as I needed to do things for me so that I felt human every so often and I would just go out and let my hair down, not on drugs just to be on the dance floor and swishing my booty was my outlet, it made me feel human and feminine.

As I write today many years after all these events[5], I can see now that it was my own inner strength that kept me going. I only wanted to get the best outcome for us all, Barry included. I was doing what I could to make sure that he got the best care, that I was not in a place to do nor give nor had the knowledge to share with him. In saying that I only wanted him to be in the care of a place that could offer the best conditions to suit his situation. I had to stay on top of it all because I had a mortgage and responsibilities, I needed a roof over my head and giving in was not the way to achieve.

I was fortunate that I had a good job and was able to attend whatever meeting I needed to survive and still be employed that was a saving grace for me; the fact that I was not penalised for it. I know the whole department knew about my situation I could tell some days when I was low there was little to no communication from others. All I needed was a friend on those days and my situation was so heavy that many could not comprehend let alone lend a hand to show empathy. I grew used to it because I totally understood, I did not like being in this place, yet, I had to cope, I needed things to stay afloat.

I had made a lot of contacts with my enquiries and eventually I made connections with a group that was in Oakleigh, Victoria. Whilst they had some vacancies, there was always a day when I could say I was coming and someone closer would get the bed in place of me. I had to work around this all the time. I started to make connection with the Matron of the

---

5   It took me 20 years to bring this story all together and sharing this personal side of me took a lot of courage – it scared me when I finally stepped towards a book launch, in looking over the book I realised how strong I had been during this journey. It was also time as I was now ready to share and to honour his 20th year since passing it seemed the most significant thing to do.

hostel, and I shared that I would come to Victoria to inspect the premise as a way of confirming a bed for Barry to move to once the paperwork had been completed. I had seven weeks of leave up my sleeve and I proceeded to use this as part of recreation and the journey to book Barry into care.

Somewhere around late September 1997, I had the thought I would need to start planning a trip to the institution in Melbourne. It was a huge task to work out before I travelled however it allowed me to be with momentum once decided I was driving to Melbourne. A confronting task, and I knew it had to be done.

All the planning and strategising took its toll on me. I was chatting online one night and met a gentleman from Canberra, he and I crossed pathways in one of the chat rooms. His name was Robert, he became a confidant and someone I could turn to when I felt so alone and frustrated from all these events. We would chat for hours online and sometimes our conversation would progress to the phone. He was a good friend and someone I trusted at the time. As time went on, he become someone who often would have me think outside the box as I could not get out of the dark hole that I felt I was in. He would challenge me to have a happy day and often asked me to bring a bounce into my next day and smile as I walked down the street. How he knew this I have no idea at the time however what transpired is that I would often think of our conversation and bring a smile to my face and pretend I had shoes with a spring and that would give me a certain bounce to my step.

I would be in a world of my own, doing this at lunchtime or just walking to and from the office morning and night. I was alive and I could do this and not feel so heavy all the time. Other days I would be walking down the street and I often felt like I was carrying so many problems that I had no idea which to attend to first. I once had a work colleague who turned out to be a confide in the office see me coming down the street and stopped me and asked what was wrong, she had heard that I was going through some issues. She did become someone who offered help while I was at work, and I did find at time she encouraged me to see things differently. I can't recall her name; all I can remember was that she was someone who had studied psychology and she seemed to understand the way in which different people handled stress. I visited her a couple of times, and she was a great comfort during some very trying times for me.

I managed to get through some days with ease and other days were so hard. It was hard to know how my day would transpire. I often felt so alone and didn't know how I would get through all of this. Meeting Robert online was a blessing as he just allowed for me to let off steam.

Chatting with Robert helped because he had a good knowledge of travel, and together, we planned my trip. I had the car serviced and tyres checked and had an extra tank of fuel on board just in case. The amount of stress I was under often prevented me from thinking with clear clarity. It was like Robert was my list and I ticked off things as I did them. The months rolled by, and the day came for me to drive out of town. I had started to say to Barry that I was going on a trip to find him the best accommodation in Melbourne. He would say "Whatever" and that he did not need accommodation. I would use this as my strategy to bring some attention to the fact that he was going to be moving to a place of better assistance because I was not fit to do this while working full time. He often said that he did not need any help, that he was fine on his own.

Awareness Wisdom Awakeners

◊ Finding people, you can confide in is one of the more pleasing things to enjoy, no judgment, no refined views, it's just good to know you can trust someone who will merely listen and be your confident. It maybe someone left field to your journey, they will show up for you.

◊ When you ask yourself, the question do your best to feel into the situation. Breath into what is being said does it feel right for you (me). Your inner soul will give you an answer, you will witness that voice in your head say yes or no! Be guided by this and ask a different question until you feel the answer is within you.

◊ It takes time to trust yourself and to witness an answer that really aligns with you. You will know the answer is right for you and you won't be swayed to go against anything that does not fit with you.

Chapter Eleven

Mindset Awareness

On the day that I started to pack my stuff into the car, Barry hovered around, following me back and forth. I had agreed to share all the LP records that we had and a reel-to-reel tape deck that was no longer in use yet still able to play. Robert was an avid collector, and he was keen to take these items off my hands, so I offered them to him to thank him for all his assistance. It was a good deal and I felt good to let go of these items as well.

I had also shared with Barry on many occasions that his trip south would be by plane however, on this day he seemed sure he was going with me. I had to say that he was to stay at home which was not an easy thing to do. My daughter was home on that day as well and she witnessed the concern on her dads' face as I drove away. From memory it was only a few minutes and he had forgotten what had happened only minutes before. I had been running on adrenaline up to this point and possibly still on, I have no idea how I managed to drive to Katherine without feeling tired, all I can say is that I got away early because I knew I had a long day's drive ahead of me, 1475 km to Alice Springs. I think I managed a good night's sleep that night and this helped me focus and stay alert.

I pulled into a trucking wayside stop just south of Katherine after 4 hours of driving and just wanted to stretch my legs and take a short break, when suddenly I was greeted by a young lad who carried a small bag and not a lot of personal belongings. He had come out of what is called the 'long grass area' on the side of the embankment. This spot was also a spot for indigenous people to camp because it was covered with trees and the long spinifex grass would hide them from sight. We chatted for a short period of time. It became evident that he had had a rough trot as his personal belongings had been stolen the night before in Darwin and he had hitched a ride with a truckie to get this far. He was on his way back to Sydney, so he was looking for a ride. I was not going to Sydney immediately however I was heading south and maybe we could connect with a truckie heading that way once we were further south. I was happy to have him as company and so we boarded the car and off we went. I can't tell you his name as I truly can't recall, he was a roaming hippie from memory, and he had made his way to Darwin for work at the time and the contract had ceased so he was heading back home to Sydney.

His wallet, as well as other personal items, was stolen at the place of accommodation, so he was staying the night before he was due to leave. I did not feel any concerns; it all seemed fair and reasonable to me. We travelled on to Alice and then on to Port Augusta and as true as you read this now, he left my car and went over the first truck he saw and as luck would have it that Truckie was heading to Sydney, so he was off on his way home with another perfectly timed hook up with a vehicle. He left his Sydney home contact details and a phone number to call when I reached Sydney as he wanted to repay me for my assistance. It was ok I had done a good deed I was happy to do that, so I never saw him again.

I had friends in Port Augusta, and I had to find them as I was due to stay a couple of nights before I headed to Canberra.

It had been arranged that I would find the large service station and they would come to meet me and then I would follow them to their home. With a couple of day's rests and feeling refreshed I started my trek across the Hay Plains a long straight road with little to no scenery of substance and a drive into the morning sun rising from the east.

I arrived in Canberra at night, it had been a long drive from Port Augusta. I was finally here my overall journey to Melbourne was almost complete, I was about 3/4s of the way there. I am not sure how I navigated my way around Canberra however something from memory tells me that Robert had shared with me a map and instructions on what roads to take and the distance to travel so it was a huge relief to make my way through a strange town at night and make it to the destination after the previous months I had been having. Robert and I had never met even though we had shared several phone conversations; it had never occurred to me to meet him.

Robert and my conversations were more involved now as we could see each other and speak in person. He was a very kind man. Our sleeping arrangements were intimate, and he was a gentleman as well. He became a very good friend during this time, and we had a few laughs and he shared with me a lot of wisdom and knowledge. He was the perfect friend I needed to have during the whole ordeal as he had also taken time off work to come with me for the purpose of doing the inspection of the hostel. It was good to have that comfort as well as the support. We spent a couple days getting to know each other and I saw a lot of sights around Canberra I had not seen before, so it was a short break before we headed to Melbourne travelling the busy Hume Highway.

My appointment with the hostel was around 1pm and it was six and half hour's drive to get to the venue allowing for additional traffic it was a good seven hours drive ahead of us.

Robert had offered for his car to be driven, he also offered to do most of the driving so that was a huge relief for me. He was a bus driver so he was used to driving long hours, a car drive would be easy or so we thought.

We made it into Melbourne with time to spare and we found the premise quite easily which was good. My meeting was a huge success, and it gave me piece of mind because I felt like I was doing the right thing for Barry, and I was happy with the environment. I recall taking the paperwork with me so that I could fax it back to the matron within a couple of weeks after I got home. I was on 7 weeks of leave, and I still had some time up my sleeve to work in for the uplift of Barry. I still had to get the doctors approval to uplift him as well.

The groundwork was done, the first steps were in place, and what a huge relief it was.

We stayed in Melbourne overnight and returned to Canberra the next morning. We ventured to my parent's place and bought them up to date, it was difficult for them to really come to terms with as Barry was of similar age to my parents and at one point, they suggested that I was dreaming this all up. It was good that Robert was there as he shared that he and I had been chatting on the phone for several months and he had heard about everything. He had been there when I was in distress and listened to my situation, he did not believe it was made-up as he shared some of his own similar situations with family members. We did not stay at my parents that night we stayed at the local motel because we wanted to leave early to head back to Canberra.

After the events of that day unfolded, I slept soundly because I felt relieved, like everything was finally coming back to its place. Robert had an early shift, so we had no time to waste. We made plans to leave early in the morning around 3am and to drive back we would be ahead of the traffic and get the major towns because we were going home through the mountain range.

We were on the road very early; I think we woke up before the alarm went off and this put us ahead of schedule. I can't recall why we drove the mountain trip back to Canberra instead of going through the Hume highway however we took this route even though it wasn't any shorter.

Robert started to drive and drove several miles before I took over the wheels, I am not sure what happened, we had been driving a reasonable amount of time now climbing up the mountain at a steady pace. I suddenly felt drowsy and fell asleep on the wheel for a few short seconds. The only thing that woke me was the corrugations in the road, they were really shaking the car. I was startled by the noise and gained complete consciousness just in time before we were about to go over the cliff. I was looking at a huge gum truck, which only seemed meters away having saw that, I turned the wheel sharply to the left and away from the edge of the cliff, losing control of traction from the loose dirt and gravel and then skidded across the road into the embankment. The car grinded and skidded a few yards before the clipping of the embankment and the corner of the car had us flip onto our side the driver's side down and the passenger's seat facing the sky. During all of this, Robert was asleep and woke with fright from the sound and the feeling he was hanging. He was strapped in the seat belt from above me. It was a little awkward and the worst part was now to get out of the car.

Robert was quick to move and protected me from the fall. I was now in shock and Robert had to really encourage me step by step to get me to climb out of my seat and climb over the console to get to the opened window now right above me. I had to pull myself up and then to jump from the window down to the ground, it was a very scary experience.

As I moved from the car, I sat on the ground wondering what had happened, we were not injured, we were just a little shaken and possibly bruised in by the ordeal. It was still dark; the sunlight had not come up and we were stuck in the mountain range heading to Cooma on the side of the road with a car flipped to its side. The new highway was not open, and we were still on the old dirt road, we did hear a couple of cars above us on the new road and they had no idea we were there.

We had no phone reception out in the mountains; we were not sure how far we had to go to the next town which was named Bombala. All we could do was wait for someone to come along and hope they stopped to help us out. I was a bit lost, as I retraced my steps on the road, I was still a bit dazzled from the impact however, I was ok and could walk so nothing really stopped me.

Remember, the tree trunk I said I could see when I came to my senses whilst driving? Well that trunk was about 50 feet up in the air and it was a very sharp fall to the creek bed at the bottom, the tree stood about 150feet tall and over 2 car lengths away from the edge of the road. With the car lights shining at the trunk, it was all I could see at that split moment. Thank goodness I had the ability to turn the wheel when I did, or I may not be here to share this story with you.

As luck would be on our side a car did come about half an hour after our incident and I got a ride to the next town Bombala. It was a sleepy town on a Saturday morning. Here I arranged for a tow truck and did the right thing and reported things to the police. Robert stayed with the car and waited for my return. By the time we had returned in the tow truck it seemed like we had lost a day. Things went well we had turned the car onto its wheels again however it was not drivable nor was it repairable. It was an old car. I had acquired a hire vehicle and it was not long before we were on our way back to Canberra a little behind in time, and we were still able to drive.

Awareness Wisdom Awakeners

◇ As the journey unfolds allow all the emotion to flow, - avoid fighting it, it's not good for you to not deal with it. You are human you are special and let your emotions show up. Cry in the shower if you want to alone and not let anyone see you. There is nothing to be ashamed of. The tears help you heal on the journey.

◇ Tears are good for the body, just do it!!!

◇ Your body will run on a certain amount of adrenaline and sooner or later when things start to change you will feel this sense of weariness overcome you. It will arrive when you least expect, and you could sleep for a while. Your body is a brilliant piece of machinery and can support you through some tough time, avoid abusing it seek for sleep and get assistance and or care for your situation. It will be the best decision you could make for your body mind and soul.

Chapter Twelve

Gaining Momentum

My journey continued. And after a few days of recuperating in Canberra and reflecting on where I was at; it was time to move on and go to the next phase of this 7-week break. My next stop was Sydney and to be honest with you it all passed very quickly the next I knew I was in Brisbane, and this is where my daughter and I re connected. She had travelled via bus into Brisbane to spend the last fortnight with me before travelling home. We had not seen each other since I left, and we needed to have some time together. My daughter and her boyfriend had a huge argument, and it was now that she called her mum to gain comfort and to gather her strength, we still had to move Barry, we still had a lot to do. I organised it all for her to board a bus and I picked her up at Roma Street bus terminal. 36 hours trip from Darwin to Brisbane direct.

With our trip completed and being back in Darwin, it was time to start to organise Barry's uplift. I had to return to work, and we had to get paperwork organised and faxed back to Melbourne for his application to be accepted and to arrange for the uplift. By now it was well into January 1998. I had been coping with Barry's situation now for 2 years. His condition had deteriorated in some ways and yet in others he was still the same person.

With the medical support behind us from the assessments, things were on track, we were ready for the uplift and got him placed into care that would be to his advantage, he would have the best care possible.

It was around this time I had someone ask me that was I doing the right thing? Did I believe it was the best outcome for Barry or it just made things easier for me? One person said, "isn't it till death do us part?", whilst Barry and I were not officially married we had lived in a de-facto relationship for so many years one could say we were married. I really was struck by this comment, it actually caused me so much more pain to come to terms with the situation of things once more. I had to determine if I gave up my job and just sat at home on welfare, I would lose my house because welfare payments did not cover my mortgage. I would lose the confidence I had fought long and hard for. I could not see why I would give it all up to be in a worse place. I felt like this was what was best for Barry and for me.

I wanted him to be in a place with the most assistance and care: I was not trained to do that, so opting to place in a home. This home just happened to be in Melbourne and that is what I focused on, getting him there safe and sound.

As time moved on, our meetings with the Alzheimer's Association grew a little more frequent as we were eligible for assistance to get Barry to Melbourne. It was in one of these meeting that we were discussing where we were up to and how far we had gone in the processing of the paperwork for the home in Melbourne. In this meeting my daughter and I were asked about who would attend the meetings. The Alzheimer's Association did not believe that young adults; teenagers needed to participate. This was not our normal meeting supervisor however we were both stunned from this question. Both my daughter and I had been at the meetings ever since we were introduced to them so why did there have to be only one person at the meeting.

They said that because I am the most senior member of our household, I needed to attend, that grandchildren did not need to come. This caused for both my daughter and I to get extremely upset. We had not broken any rules, we were there because we genuinely needed assistance and there was no one else we could turn to. This caused for both my daughter and I to be very annoyed, we told them that Barry was the father of this child, and I was the mother it was not a grandparent situation, nor was it that Barry was my parent. It was obvious that the representative had not read the information and was accusing us of misleading them. In a normal situation yes, a grandparent or child did not need to be at the meetings for a grandparent. However, in this case whilst Barry was old enough to be a grandparent, he was the father of the child, and she was entitled to hear what steps we needed to take for the wellbeing of her father. I was the partner of the person in question so as the senior adult and legal partner of the client it was right for me to be at the meetings, this caused for some very heated words at the time.

I know I took the legal paperwork with me to the next meeting which was the birth certificate with Barry as the father and my daughter as the legitimate child. This caused some tension during a few meetings because we did not feel like we were being heard, at this stage and we ended up talking to the overall manager of the Association in his office to dissolve this issue.

When we did get back on track it was made quite clear that the assistance to us would be for just me as the senior member of the family, we understood this and accepted the assistance, we were not there for the both of us to gain anything other than guidance and support.

By now the days were moving towards February and we were in constant connection with the hostel for a position available to uplift Barry. For about 6 weeks, we did this regularly. I had reached a stage where I had to spend several nights away from the house. It was the only way I could stay in control. Sometimes, my daughter would be with her boyfriend or at a girlfriend's place, sleeping over. We coped this way and it worked for us. We would visit the house daily to check in and see what was happening. Even though I was paying for everything, I still had a responsibility to check on Barry, though his condition never changed. It was very cold being around him, I had to sleep in a camping bed. It was a hard decision to make, yet it was the best step to take to keep my sanity.

As March '98 approached, we were advised that the timing for uplift was getting closer. It was all in the communication with the Alzheimer's Association for support in the purchase of airfare and the packing of the items for Barry's case. It was good to pack for him because he put so many unnecessary things in. It was recommended not to pack too many personal belongings. His room would be small, and he would not have room for big items. A couple of pictures for his wall and that was about it. I had to repack his bag several times and keep it separate until the actual day of the uplift.

The air ticket was paid, and confirmation had been made we now had an uplift date for Barry to travel, little did we know our first stumbling block was now to get Barry out of the house as he dug his heels in saying he was not going anywhere. It was the 6th of March, and we were due to board the plane at around 7am in the morning Barry was not moving and we needed to be at the airport soon.

I can't recall exactly what happened, however my girlfriend Toni was with us for support even though she could not get Barry to move, it was a very difficult few minutes before we could get him to the car for our trip to the airport.

An arrival to the airport there was still several steps to get to the plane. Getting inside the airport was one thing now we also faced too many people in the airport and Barry wanted to leave. It took a bit of convincing however finally we were where we needed to be to board the plane. I contacted one of the airhostesses and she was able to bring us to the front of the line so we could get settled on the plane for our trip.

What I was to witness happen was like an inner child in Barry started to shine as he was on the big plane first and he was fascinated with the books and things in the pocket of the seat in front of us. We were about the middle of the plane he had a window seat, so he was interested to watch what was going on outside whilst the balance of passenger loaded the plane.

I can't begin to know what was happening for my daughter at this time and during this time, A very hard place to witness. She was going to be saying goodbye to her dad. It was a difficult time for anyone however for my daughter she was witnessing the demise in her dad and to be now watching him ushered down the tunnel towards the plane was a huge loss for any child, let alone see your dad disappear. She was saying a farewell to her dad as this is a huge emotional strain on any one and the state of mind.

It was a very deep sad moment for us both.

Her dad was truly not fully aware of the impact it was having on her and me as well. I was sad to have to leave her at the airport and yet it was something that had to be done. Tears streamed down our cheeks; this parting was not easy a cruel part of life for anyone to witness. At 16 yrs of age how do you digest that, and unfortunately, I was on the plane, my girlfriend was the only one to attend to my daughter currently. I know you are reading this and say why couldn't she go with me. The Alzheimer's Association would only pay for one ticket one person to accompany the patient, and it was all arranged through a govt agency for this too occur. We had had a discussion around this, and it was decided that only I would go. My daughter come to her own resolution on this matter.

Sad and all as it were, the journey was only beginning; with the tears as what was to unfold was more devastating to witness in my life that nobody should have to endure.

Our plane trip was good. During the time Barry was in a childlike manner and seemed to be excited the hostesses come through sometimes pushing the button to get their attention, finally a hostess gave us some headphones and Barry was content to listen to the channels on the plane as the 4-5 hour journeyed to Melbourne.

Arriving in Melbourne was only a part of the trip of this whole process; the meeting of my parents was a little difficult as Barry was a little unsure of their names and yet in some ways you could tell he knew them just not sure where he knew them from. It was arranged that my parents would meet us at the airport, and we could be driven to the place of destination for Barry to settle into.

This was not an easy decision to come to, I had to weigh up all the pros and cons of the place and to identify if this was going to be a good fit for Barry to manage as best, he could. I had several long phone conversations with different matrons of different hostels and with the help and guidance from a medical profession in one of the govt agencies all associated with the Alzheimer's Association in Darwin. This took some courage and some defined strength to even be able to work it all out. I had a couple of friends I could talk to and my daughter who was a great help despite being a teenager and for all she was witnessing. I was grateful for her maturity to discuss all of this. Most teenagers would want to be out parting and dancing however this situation was turned upside down for my daughter as it was her dad we were managing at this time.

Awareness Wisdom Awakeners

◇ When it came time to make this decision, I can't recall who the person was that sat with me and assisted the amount of paperwork that was needed. As the main file on the patient was with this person it seemed a blessing that they were able to help. If a family member can't help, I feel confident to say that administrative assistance will be there to guide you. They understand what the journey is life for the member of the family trying to manage it all.

◇ It's time for all the information to flow through your brain and understand the impact of what you are managing. Your life can be like having to run two lives to get one life sorted then you can align your life to be in flow again. It's tough I get it however there is always some help to guide you on this journey.

Chapter Thirteen

6th March Changed Direction

Nothing could have prepared me... Getting to Melbourne was one thing settling Barry into the new accommodation arrangements was another.

Our arrival and collecting of luggage were all good, there was a small amount of chatter and Barry still a bit amazed by the numbers of people as we walked from the airport to the car ready to travel through Melbourne. We had a good hour to go via car. Our destination on the southside of Melbourne. What surprised us all as we drove through the different streets is that Barry would be so coherent and acknowledge different landmarks of Melbourne as if he was there yesterday. This was amazing, he even noticed that an old building had been pulled down and asked what happened to it as clear as he could, however with the conversation over, he was not aware of what he had merely shared only moments ago and so the journey to the venue we reached with several ahh haa moments of Barry's awareness and clarity even if for a short period of time.

Barry grew up in Melbourne and spent a lot of time as a Taxi driver at some point of his life and he was also a mechanic at a Coffee packaging business on the south side of Melbourne.

The arrival at the gates of the premise was where things began to change. None of us expecting to witness what we did.

For a lucid moment as dad drove straight into the premise Barry shouted out, "I'm not going here"

The wording on the gateway was noted and he only saw the words of Mental Institute as noted underneath was The Aged Care Facilities for over 60's. Wording I had not even witnessed before this moment as being a cognitive point that registered for him. So, this was a new experience. In all his previous cognitive assessments around reading and knowing of anything in society or news events his answer was "don't know don't care don't want to know". So, it had been noted that he didn't show any interest in society events, and this was assumed part of the steps for the illness.

On arrival at the doorway of the facility I was greeted by the nurse of the day, and she shared his room was all set up and we could move him to room number 338, I can't remember the actual number because he never made it to the door of the premise. Barry had other ideas of what was going to happen, and he was adamant he was not going inside the building.

He sat in the car whilst I was inside finalising everything it may have been a maximum of 15 mins could have been less. I was to arrive back at the car to a very agitated man who was now trying to open the boot of the car, to which dad held the lock on the keypad and Barry was getting a little angry he could not get to his things. He was adamant he was not going inside the building. Mum became somewhat emotional as she had not witnessed any of this and dad was trying to be supportive of me and in the end stepped away as he was not able to manage Barry either.

All I could do was talk to him and be as rationale as I could. This was not working either. Finally, dad opened the boot and Barry dived on his 2 bags. He proceeded to take a few things out and then grabbed the lighter one and started walking towards the gate we came in by.

Confusion reigned. It was a little heated as Barry was a very stubborn man as well and he was off; nothing was going to stop him. Mum ran after him and tried to calm him down she got him to turnaround and by this time the nurse from the premise was at the car seeing if we had a problem. Barry had meandered back to the car and said to the nurse I'm not staying here and again turned and walked at right angles to the original plan he was following. This was a little easier as he moved to the front yards of the open grassland of the property and only went as far as the street fence. Not overly high. Jumpable with effort.

My nightmare began here. My loss truly began here. My misunderstanding began here. I was witnessing a huge impact on a man that seemed so scared and alone yet unsure of what he could do.

I witnessed Barry pace the fence line repeatedly. I did everything I could to bring some resolution to the man so he could see it was a no-win situation. I did as best I could to ask him to stay calm and talk with me. He would stare at me with a piercing gaze I could tell the man was angry, lost and confused, where to go. I must have been out the front trying to calm him down for what could have been half an hour maybe more and I was trying to manage on my own. I can't recall which parent I think my mum came to me to see if it was having any success and all I could say to her were words of distress please ask the front desk for some help!

She proceeded to the office and then went back to sit in the car park to wait for me to return. Someone from the hostel did arrive outside at the grassed area, and they witnessed the distress and trauma in Barry and was not able to calm him either, so it seemed huge task to settle him. I think someone bought some water for Barry and he stopped to drink this only not for long and he was pacing the fence line again. The representative went back inside and the next I know there was a man on the scene he was from the security. I wanted to breath a sigh of relief as now hopefully there was an experienced person to help.

How wrong was I; this man I feel aggravated the situation even more?

I was able to gain Barry's attention and he came to meet the security man and with heated words told me to "f-off" and to leave him alone he was not going to this venue and that was that.

Our heated words of desperation lead me to a point of tears of despair. Here I was trying to do the best I could to calm Barry, no experience, and no depth of total appreciation what I had to do or could do and what was happening, and his anger towards me left me in a devastating place of pain and emotional distress.

The security guard followed Barry back and forth and in the end the security guard lost sight of Barry for a split second and Barry was gone. Over the fence totally out of sight. I too in all my tears did not see the event happen to be able to follow him. I know I was a tad weak at the knees we had lost him. The road was a huge intersection and busy all the time. All the security man could say was he got away from me.

I looked up the street and across the street, it was to no avail Barry had jumped the fence and crossed the road we think to be among the maze of buildings and people on the other side of the street. We could see rather clearly up and down the street on the hostel side. Nothing resembled a person. He had just vanished.

I walked back the point of arrival and shared that Barry had jumped the fence and the security guard could not locate him. My parents by now had been sitting here a good 4-5 hours feeling a bit distraught at all the things that had happened. I was exhausted not only from the immense pressure this was however at the depth of the impact this was now having on me from a new perspective. I don't recall how long it was until the police arrived all I recall is looking in the bags in the boot to find a family photo that I had put in for Barry to have and bring this out to have some identification to the police. What an experience to witness what an horrific day to watch unfold.

6th March could it get any worse?...

With the arrival of the police, it was next to note that they wanted to interview me regarding Barrys disappearance. This took place in one of the interviewing rooms in the hostel general office area. No idea of the names of the sergeants I think they were all I know is I told them the truth of what had happened and the impact it had had on Barry for this time.

Barry was now a missing person of Victoria around 5 hours since he arrived in the state from his trip from Darwin.

What was to transpire really gutted me on some level I will do my best to say it as it happened in the interview room with the police, myself, and the security guard. No real names are being used.

"Sargent John, here can you please identify yourself?"

Yes, I am Steve from the security firm based in Melbourne.

"How long have you been in security Steve?"

"About 2 yrs Sargent"

"When were you alerted to the situation here at the Hostel?"

"About 4 hours ago Sargent"

"Did you feel you were in control of the situation Steve?"

"I believed I was initially Sir"

"Was the person in distress getting calmer or more distraught?"

"He was getting more distraught, Sargent"

"When you are in a place of a patient in distress what are you supposed to do, Steve?"

"I am supposed to call for back-up" "I did call the office of the hostel and to find no further security was available"

"Steve did you call for further backup"

"No, I did not"

"When you are in need of help what are you supposed to do Steve in an emergency situation like you had today"

"I am supposed to call for back up and I didn't feel I needed to" I felt I was in control Sargent"

"Obviously Steve you were not in control, the patient is now missing Steve" Is there any reason why you did not call for back up Steve"

"No, I felt I was handling the manner properly. Sargent"

"Well, it's very obviously you have failed and will possibly be with a loss of licence from this matter."

Thank you, Steve, we have no further Questions.

End of interview

Barry was well and truly missing.

Not the desired outcome I was working towards.

Chapter Fourteen

Stunned, Unsure what Happens Next

T**he** hour of the day now getting closer to late in the afternoon. The afternoon was getting a bit chilly, and tears started to roll down my face more now as it was realised that Barry did not have a jacket or jumper on, nor did he have any money on him. This whole event really started to point out the impact of what had happened on this day 6th March.

I had followed the instructions from the hostel regarding what clothing was need packed and what had small number of memorabilia for Barry to be placed in his room. Now only the bags would make it to the room nothing else. Barry was missing. The police were aware of the situation and proceeded to let us know they would do everything they could to keep a watchful eye out in the days to come to find Barry.

It was of little comfort, here he was in the busy southside of Melbourne in a suburb called Oakleigh and many people in the region. Finding one person was going to be like finding a needle in a haystack. Nobody really knew which way he went initially so it was hard to know where to start. We thanked the police and as we bundled into the car for our journey towards Wonthaggi, we still had around 1.5 hours road trip to reach my parents' home.

I think I was a bit numb; I knew I felt sad and, in some discomfort, yet life still had to move on. By the time we left the hostel and gathered our thoughts it was getting close to 6pm and we were on our way home. Mum and dad decided to stop on the way to grab a bit to eat at one of the country hotels. It would be well and truly dark when we would arrive at Wonthaggi, and I was to catch a plane back to Darwin next morning as organised from the Alzheimer's Association it was a trip for Barry's placement. Nothing had prepared us for the outcome we had witnessed.

I know I slept well that night despite being up early the next morning to be at the airport by 11am I think it was. On the journey to the airport there was a point of clarity as I had missed read my flight ticket and we were sitting in the traffic, and I realised my flight time was going to be around 30 mins earlier than I had shared. With all the impact of the events that had occurred I was not thinking straight and the impact of the events I read the wrong time scheduled for my flight.

Oh, my lord this put some pressure on dad as the driver as we were in a lot of traffic that was early morning congestion and the sign on the freeway read 45 mins to Airport. As you can imagine this set up a lot of tension in the car. I sat in the back and dad and mum exchanged words of heated explanation!!! I just kept praying for a break in traffic to reach the plane.

Our goodbyes at the airport were basically non existent and it was to get out of the car grab my carry-on bag and run. From memory I had a few minutes to spare so I reached the plane flight.

What I wasn't prepared for was the on burst of tears and emotion that would flood me on the plane and thank goodness I was able to gain a seat on my own. The first hostess was wonderful as she bought me a box of tissues and a bag to dispose of them. She comforted me most of the trip. When she heard part of the event that had happened, she was so comforting on this journey. The realisation of the events and the hesitancy of the boarding of the plane all happened so quickly. I don't recall I got to really say goodbye there was no time for a hug to my parents and I don't recall if I said thank you for all they had done. So much stress on my mind with the loss of Barry still out on the streets. My mind was in so much pain and emotional hurt from this whole event. I had 5 hours on the plane to Darwin. I had done everything I could I had prepared him for this trip the best I could however I was not prepared for the impact that the disappearance of Barry would have on me as well.

Arrival back in Darwin saw a huge flood of tears as I shared the journey with my daughter on everything as I had recalled and what the impact had for me.

I had a much bigger headache in Darwin as my new house had just witnessed rain and it leaked at most corner points of the house, so I was dealing with the builder and insurance as to why this was happening. What a nightmare this on top of the other had on me. I called a girlfriend to be with me as I was in no state to answer many questions, yet I needed to get the house leak fixed as more rain was on the forecast and I only had a few days to get this sorted.

The insurance company acted quickly they were at my home within a matter of hours, and I was able to give them all they needed to get the house repaired. Little did I know that the builder had cut a corner in building my home and never placed any wet weather webbing in the right places and so it caused so many anxious moments.

My house had been cladded so it was a case of all cladding to be removed and webbing in place and then the house would be sealed with no more leakages. What it meant inside the house was to move all the furniture to the middle so that the workers could reach where they needed from the inside and repair what water damage I had and most of the work also occurred on the outside with all the cladding removed. It was a good week of impact for sure.

One may be asking how you cope with all this tension and emotional impact? I can't answer you specifically all I can say is that within me was a strength I had never known, and I drew on this as each situation occurred.

The searching of Barry happened all at the same time, whilst the house was being repaired.

By now it was Monday the 9th of March and if memory serves me correctly it was then known as Labour Day in Melbourne, and they had a holiday on this day. By now I had rung the police station a couple of times and to no avail had any news of them finding Barry. I lived in hope all the time.

My stress load had me at the Doctor to gain a few days off work. I was mainly in tears, a good part of the time. I was hurting and feeling into the pain of having left Barry in such a difficult state as I had to return to Darwin. Its not a very good feeling to deal with and nor was it comfortable to speak about as it always left me in a lot of tears. This whole journey pushed me and pulled me to a level I never knew about for life. Having support from family was difficult as they were all in Melbourne, I was in Darwin 3500 miles away. I did not have anyone who could offer respite to have a Janice day to reflect. I found ways around this in small, short hours where I could help me cope.

I had let all the departments know that Barry was missing, and I had been in contact with folks at the Alzheimer's Association, so everyone that needed to know was now aware of the situation.

I had been in contact with the police station as well and was alarmed to be told that I was to stop calling as there were too many calling the station on several occasions to ask of Barrys situation if found yet.

I don't know what come over me however the policeman on the other end of the phone was not expecting the outburst of profanities and words of explosion that erupted from me as being the person of most to be calling having him Barry as my partner that I had delivered to Melbourne, on Friday be the only person to be making the calls and that I was the only person of contact to be contacted when the man had been found. Have I made myself clear sir, I gave him my number and said to note that as the only person to contact? I am the persons next of kin and guardian in this situation. Do you hear me I shouted at the man on the other end of the phone?

I was livid. I was shaking, how much worse could this get?

I recall putting the phone down and dropping to the floor so alarmed and so distressed with what had happened.

My daughter helped me from the floor and to gain some composure of the incident. I was shaking and a tad annoyed from this experience, I recall having a drink of water to rehydrate myself from losing so many tears. I was feeling exhausted. It was hot and I was sweating from the heat externally. From the conversation with the policeman, it appeared there were several others calling and unbeknownst to me the last update had been given to a stranger I had no idea of where they had come from.

About an hour later...

I made a call to the station only to find out that Barry had been found and that he was now in care and the searching would cease. I asked why nobody called me the carer guardian of this person, and the policeman said he was not aware. I didn't have the strength to go over it all again however I was able and savvy to ask who was told of his being found. He answered with this name of the person I did not know and that he was found about an hour ago. I said thank you and tears just streamed down my face streamed at an alarming rate. I was short of breath I was relieved, and I was heart broken it was now just on 4 days since he was missing. He was found and I had no idea who this person was that had the information. Why wasn't I told? Why wasn't I the point of call the police to let me know? I have asked my self this several times over the years and in the next coming event I was to witness that the family knew also and had not had the courtesy to let me know either.

No body knows that feeling of not having been told of your partner being found, that gutted feeling that everyone else knew and no consideration how to tell me.

Nobody knew of my angst moments of what I was going through and what I was feeling. Suddenly, they all cared and did not have any respect or consideration to tell me. I ask my self why and what does it mean to have family if you are treated like this.

They knew I was distressed from it all or they had their own interpretation of the events of what I had done to get this situation to be resolved. Nobody asked to help me nobody shared any consideration. It was years later I worked out they held a grudge against for all my actions they all saw it as

I did the wrong things. Yes, they never walked in my shoes. Not once, now many years later a sister has worked in aged care and dementia, she may have some consideration to this journey however no real depth of appreciation to the pain I suffered and the journey I witnessed to manage to get Barry to a place of care. What a huge upheaval and distortion on this whole matter. Coping with Alzheimer's is a solo journey and one that teaches you so many things about others appreciation.

In letting that out I feel so much better and will continue. It's been too long held inside it needed a venting.

Now back to finding out where Barry was found...

I had made some composure to ring my mum, maybe she did not know, well how different a story was I to learn.

Mum shared of Barry being found, she had no explanation of why I was not told, she just thought I would know WRONG! I also shared that I had no idea of this person who supposedly had the confirmation from the police. She replied it was correct and so the chain of events unravelled on Barry being found. I know I did express that I thought she would have been more with compassion to let me know an hour ago, she didn't know how I would respond!!!

Awareness Wisdom Awakeners

◊ Sometimes our closest members of family have no idea how we will react. It is allowed as you are the one going through the turmoil there is no right or wrong way to deal with it. Let your body do what it must do it's your best coping method. Being mindful of how you feel its all part of being able to let go on some level. The pain is real.

◊ Everybody will have their perspective of what is happening however you are the one in the middle of all of this. You are allowed to yell and scream to release some endorphins from your body, and you are allowed to feel the situation. Nobody else has the right to judge you in any way.

Chapter Fifteen

Finding Barry

Barry seemed to have survived the 3 nights of the cold and here he was in the 4th day and being found. Nobody not even Barry could share where he spent the previous nights. The only thing that was obvious was he was still able to smell out a BBQ burning, and this is where he was identified, and the police were called.

In Barry's past he had lit and stoked and worked on a BBQ on many events and outings he attended. As a Tour coach driver, he would help with the cooking on the BBQ, so it was not strange to me to hear he had been lured to an open BBQ, as a place to seek something. He was hungry and the smell of sausages and onions would have been a great combination.

Let me share here, Barry's escape from the hostel happened in a place called Oakleigh and just by chance this was close to the neighbouring suburbs in which he grew up in. There is speculation here and its only my opinion, if Barry was able to recognise the places in the city as we drove to this hostel, what are the chances he knew the road he was on, and this was his escape from the hostel. It has been a pondering on my mind for many years. Did Barry have a moment of recollection he was in a place he recognised from his younger years.

Now to add to this, his home address he grew up in was Park Street, Middle Park. How coincidental was it that Barry was eventually found in Park Street Oakleigh A tennis tournament on Labour Day was being held and he smelt the cooking of sausages and found himself gaining a feed and being found as such.

As things rolled on the person in the club knew that something was wrong and started to ask some questions when they realised, he was not cognitive with responses they were suspicious he could be missing from a family.

What happened was as I understand from the information that was shared to me. Barry had on his normal cap he would wear and unbeknownst to many he had a piece of paper inside the rim that when he took his hat off inside the venue a piece of paper fell out of the hat's rim.

In 1998, yes, they did have mobile phones and one of the organisers of the Tennis event rang the mobile number on the piece of paper. He was not aware that the number would head to Darwin and contact Barrys day carer who had been assigned to him whilst I was working. He was aware of the situation, and he contacted the Alzheimer's Association in Darwin to advise of his findings. The carer advised that it was wise to contact the Oakleigh Police station as this was where he was first reported missing.

With this information it was not long before the police were able to collect Barry and take him to get a physical at the Monash Hospital and then he was transported to the hostel for his care to start.

As nobody was able to identify Barry, he spent a good couple of days in hospital. Mum and Dad were the only ones to be able to recognise him and confirm to the hospital and the police that he was the right man for identification purposes. I know he was given another psych assessment, and this shared the degree of his condition and what the next step of action would be for Barry.

All I know is this happened and the next I am receiving a call from the hostel to say that Barry was now safe in a room in the Hostel and being cared for.

Awareness Wisdom Awakeners

◇ Sometimes family may have to be called in to do the difficult situations, as there may times when an outside person needs to be the identifying. Person to recognise the actual person. There may be variables of where this may happen, this for me was also hard, yet it defined a moment that finally Barry was getting to the place of care that was originally sourced.

◇ The upheaval for the person in the middle of this I can only imagine is huge. I know what I witnessed from my experience, always allow for all the variables to flow, it's a very hard journey when it is witnessed.

Chapter Sixteen

Escaped from Hostel

Barry was an escape artist. He has left the premise a couple of times in the first place, and this raised concerns for his well-being and care and after getting out these couple of times it was next to go to the next level of security care. He spent 4-5 years in accommodation and by his 66th birthday he was into the 3rd level of accommodation hostels as clever Barry had kept escaping.

He was clever enough to work out a keypad to unlock the door and he gained access and was found at a local shopping centre on one occasion.

It was at this third centre I think it was that my daughter was able to visit him. There had been a few interruptions and finding her half brother and sharing the journey with him, has allowed these two siblings to build rapport and eventually they went to visit their dad in care.

The 1st son had visited his dad and it was here that he realised that the man in front of him was his dad.

Barry had taught his youngest daughter to tie her shoelaces and on a visit for the 1st son to see his dad he witnessed the experience of him tying his shoes. This was a very important point for the son. All his life he had struggled with why he tied his shoelaces in a different way to other kids. The evidence was now in front of him.

Barry was predominately left-handed, so he tied his laces left over right instead of right over left. The laces were done up only the result was a little different. The son witnessed that he as the child had been taught by his dad to tie all his laces left over right and he still did all his life. It was a bit of a chuckle once he realised that Barry's youngest daughter also did the same. This gave a very connecting and unique relationship for the two of them. Barry's first son has since passed, and I acknowledge the son here as he was the spitting resemblance of his father and I honour 1st son with all dignity and respect.

It was shared to me close to the end of Barrys life that he was such a gentleman and such a sweetheart to manage and care for. One of the carer's rang me personally to share her condolences to me when he had passed.

As I continue here, I share an acknowledgement to my daughter as she witnessed everything with me. She was my rock; she was my comforter when no one else was around to be of comfort.

She was such a great support, and I truly am grateful for what she and I shared with each other on this journey.

 Thank you, Daughter

She was suffering in her own way as she was dealing with her own pain of losing her dad. Sometimes this never crossed my mind as I could only feel my pain and it caused tension with us deeply. I recall one day we both broke into each other's arms as we knew it was one hell of a road to be on. We had tolerated each other's pain and nothing more we could do yet to cry for each other.

We were standing in the middle of the now fixed house and we both realised it was a release of tensions for us both. Hearing of dad's (Barry) escaping was always a concern for us as we had no way of doing anything now, he was in the care of the hostel. They would ring us and let us know when he was out and when he was placed back into care. Sometimes at that higher restriction.

This story the truth of the journey will be a shock on some level. It will wrench you as to the way in which I was told of his passing. Nothing can prepare you for this information regardless of how it comes to you.

So, the ending is not easy nor is it untruthful.

It is exactly as I witnessed.

Barry had kept good health all his life, the diagnosis of this disease was the hardest to witness and to gain a greater understanding of what was happening. A journey of awareness and clarity that we can never know what is happening on the inside of the body nor what is happening in the mind. All I know for sure is we never die of Alzheimer's Dementia; we die of an ailing other part of the body that breaks down or stops working. Nothing can tell us that Alzheimer's is the cause of this either. What is yet to be established is what is the cause of this disease what makes the internal of the brain to break down. My personal feeling and mine alone is the impact of too much sugar, artificial sugar in our body. Smoking from an early age has its impact as well. These are just my thoughts nothing in science has proven what it is in being diagnosed with Alzheimer's Dementia.

Awareness Wisdom Awakeners Epilogue

◇ This journey is not easy. It takes a lot of courage, and strong will to manage a situation as like this. If one of the biggest lessons I could take away from this experience is what anybody else thinks is none of my business, I am only responsible for myself in the first instance to stay alert for the member who is witnessing this experience and that is all that truly matters.

◇ What someone else thinks are happening is just that 'thinks it is happening' the only 2 people who know are the ones in the middle of the experience. In my case my daughter as well.

◇ The point of this whole journey has been to share an experience for what I endured and to share that whilst not an everyday experience, there could have been more anger and more pain or there could have been an adult regress back to childhood days. What I aim to share is that this is very real and like in all humans there are so many variables as to how this will appear for you. Trust your intuition and truly be open to witness the changes that occur. Your experience will be unique as was mine.

◇ God bless All ...

Conclusion 4th Sept 2022

The telephone mobile rings: it's around 5.50 am...

Hello,

Is this Janice Muir

Yes, who is calling?

It nurses Barb from Oakley Hospital Emergency ward

Barry has had a heart attack

Oh, hang on ...

He is dead!

The phone hung up and I was left half awake, stunned, and

unsure what I had just heard.

Barry had passed away.

Eulogy

Eulogy of Barry Muir, compiled by his daughter and Janice.

Barry Alexander Muir's life thou troubled was lived to the fullest, he enjoyed meeting and helping people and most of all he enjoyed traveling. He drove tour coaches around Australia, had traveled to Ayres Rock 7 times but never climb the lump of sandstone in the middle of the desert as he so described it.

His life had many facets to it which there is no recollection, and some of which he never spoke of and others that were great joys, but for me my dad was always there when I needed him and always a friend to talk to.

Dad moved to Darwin in the late sixties, and he fell in love with the country and the people of the Northern Territory. He worked in the Angliss meat works at the Darwin Abattoirs for a couple of years, and he is one of, if not the only person to have ice skated in Darwin, due to the meat freezer icing over. He also drove for Darwin Bus and Motor Services in Darwin in the tourist industry, traveling the unsealed and out back terrain of the NT. In 1974, he experienced and witnessed one of Australia's natural tragedies Cyclone Tracey. He lived in a 5-story apartment block known as the Mansion flats that still stands in Darwin today, as they were one of the tallest buildings in 1974, he told the story of the wall hanging that always fell whenever anyone walked past it, yet the strongest wind did not blow that wall hanging down during the cyclone Tracey.

Dad's keenness to get things back on track, and whilst working for the bus company, saw Dad transport people to and from the Darwin Airport during the mass evacuation after the devastation of Tracey hitting Darwin. Now, 2 yrs later he felt the need to move on from there and moved back to Melbourne where he drove tour coaches out of Dandenong for about 12 months. It was on one of these tour coach journeys that Dad's life met my mum, Jan. Dad had the burn and desire to return to Darwin so in 1977 Mum and Dad headed off towards Darwin. Dad was fortunate that friends he had from when he previously lived in Darwin knew of his skills and he was lucky to find work at the then Stokes Hill Power Station, where he worked as a Foreman with approximately twenty-two apprentices under his command. He held this job for a period of 9yrs 11months and 2 weeks exactly, until he was re-trenched, and the power station closed. The retrenchment saw him move to Mackay in Central Qld that was in 1987.

In 1982, Dad's life changed again with me, his "little kid", arrival into the world and it was a proud moment, cigars were issued all round. I brought a new lease of life to him as he found himself in the role of dad at 47. My memories of Dad were that he was a diligent person that would try to help anyone in need. I remember one of the first time I heard my dad laugh was when I came home from school with a silly song and sitting in the back of our car I started singing at the top of my voice, he watched in the rearview mirror until I finished and then burst out laughing. That is one of my most precious memories. He was always there when I needed someone to talk to and whenever my science projects were running late.

In 1984 we lived in the rural areas of Darwin, and he was a keen volunteer, for the local bush fire brigade. At one bush fire, a freak flash of wind caused a fireball to engulf the truck that Dad was operating from, and he was severely burnt to his hands and face. He was operating the hose, and this was proven to be the only thing that saved him from being burnt more severely as he pointed the hose totally on himself. The exposed areas of his hands were burnt so badly that he had skin grafts from his leg to heal the back of his hands.

The move to Mackay in 1987 also saw some changes in life for Dad as well, he found himself unemployed for long periods of time, until he located work at Mackay TAFE College where he was employed as the maintenance fitter then promoted as the manager of facilities with 18 cleaning staff, 1 carpenter, and numerous other staff under his control. A job he aptly managed well.

He also managed with Mum a small Orchid nursery on our property where he dabbled and fertilized the orchids and flowers, a love he enjoyed a lot. He proved this love by helping to found with mum and nine others the Pioneer River Orchid and Plant Association aka the PROPA Club. The club is now in its fifteenth year and still going strong, with Dad's founding commitment as president for the first 7 years the club had concrete grounding that has kept it alive to date.

He then found himself on another trek back to Darwin in 1994 (in search of the elusive perfect orchid) and again the burning desire to return was eminent. Mum, Dad, and I packed up our belongings and moved back to Darwin in 1995.

By '96 there were signs that Dad's working life was becoming harder to cope with and in 1997 his health was changing, and he became a very depressed man. His ability to communicate became difficult and he was beginning to be very forgetful. By the time I was sixteen there were signs that Dad no longer recognized me and in 1998 he was assessed with the disease Alzheimer's dementia and was no longer of sound mind. In 1999 Mum had no other option but to place Dad in fulltime residential care in Melbourne as facilities to cater for him were not available in Darwin. Dad, Mum, and I enjoyed a happy family life with lots of travel and adventure camping with fishing for the elusive barramundi being one of Dads favorite past times.

It was unfortunate that it was Dad's choice to not identify himself as the father of Bryan, Andrea, and Jackie, when they tried to contact him in the early 1990's. After discussion of reconciliation with his past children took place between Mum and Dad, and it caused some tension to which, Dad requested that the topic never be spoken about again. I was to learn of the other part of Dad's life through a slip of the tongue from my parent's solicitor, which when I was 15 years old identified that I had a half-brother and two half-sisters.

It was a shame that Dad elected not to introduce us for himself, it took me 2 years and a large amount of courage for me to make that first contact, but with the failing of dad's health and advice from medical experts I made contact and advised his past family of his move to Melbourne and declining health. At that point in time there was little anyone could do to reconcile.

With the passing of time and the loss of Dad's life there is little I can say to ease the hurt and the pain in which he suffered. Having been a man with so much knowledge about Australia and the engineering world in which he worked it would have been hard for him to have coped with the loss of his life and memories. I hope that with his passing it has shown that you should not hold grudges forever.

Spoken by Barry's Youngest Daughter

REST IN PEACE

17.12.1935 - 4.9.2002

CPSIA information can be obtained
at www.ICGtesting.com
Printed in the USA
BVHW012348010922
646127BV00005B/19